AKELDAMA

~

By

Kristine Lowder

AKELDAMA

~

By Kristine Lowder

Published by
Living Stones Fellowship International
P.O. Box 103
Warrens, Wisconsin 54666
www.lsfi.org

ISBN: 978-1-885054-74-6

Akeldama is a book rich in descriptions of Bible history. If there is one thing I want when I read a book, it is to feel as if I am there, tasting every taste, smelling every scent on the breeze and, yes, even feeling the agonizing emotions that the characters are feeling. Through *Akeldama* I experienced the forgiveness, the healing power and the heartbreak that each woman who encountered Christ felt. I could place myself in their lives and sing the Hallel right along with them! Thank you, Kristine Lowder, for allowing me to encounter Christ in such a powerful way.

- Joyce Cunningham, Director, Child Evangelism Fellowship
Pacific Harbors, Washington

I have read only a few Christian novels worthy of the name. My favorite Christian authors are C.S. Lewis, Stephen R. Lawhead, Joseph F. Girzone, and now Kristine Lowder. I must tell you that her book, *Akeldama*, touched me so deeply that I cried like a baby as I read the final chapter. Yes, the final chapter is about the resurrection of Jesus Christ—not a new subject. But something in her telling of it blessed me with joy, gratitude, awe, and wonder. I cannot remember a time when I wanted to re-read a book as soon as I finished it. *Treat yourself to a great book!*

- William C. Oakes, Senior Pastor, Living Stones Fellowship
Warrens, Wisconsin

Anyone familiar with the New Testament has read about the miracles Jesus performed. But what about the people on the receiving end? What was it like for them to live in that time? Who did they think this Man was

In Akeldama, author Kristine Lowder weaves a tapestry tale of mystery, intrigue, compassion, longing, and truth as she brings to vivid life three women with deep aches and needs, mysterious pasts, and hopes for the future we can all recognize.

Who is this Man? That is the question each of them wrestled with as they witnessed his healing touch--and then witnessed his seemingly senseless death on the cross.

Who is this Man? It's the question each of us must answer for ourselves. Akeldama brings the Gospel message closer to home and challenges us no to set it down without having reached our own conclusion.

Kristine Lowder is a gifted writer with an ability to put the reader in the scene. Be prepared to spend a few hours in Jerusalem, first century A.D.

- Peggy Matthews Rose, Collaborative Writer and Editor
Orange County, California

Akeldama is an historical novel. The action takes place within an historical setting and represents an honest attempt based on considerable research to tell a story set in the past. Characters may be real or fictional. Recognizable geographic locations, personalities and main events within this novel are based on the biblical record and additional extra-biblical sources. Other events as well as background are the products of the author's imagination.

To Chris

~~~

If the sands of earth's shores
melted each time
my heart and mind turn to you,
the whole world would be beachless.

and to

Yeshua of Nazareth
~~~

Dei Gratia

Prologue

Vile. Wretched. Worthless. Synonymous for all that was foul and polluted in Palestine, perhaps in the whole earth.

Parched and blistered under a scorching Palestinian sun, the valley lay like a shriveled snake shed in the languid light of dawn. The valley's lower part bordered Yerushalayim on the south and became the wadi *er-Rababi* near its junction with the ravine of Kidron. The ground had long been surrendered to burial purposes, specifically as a burial place for strangers. Clawing the south sides of the infamous Valley of Hinnom near the outermost part of the vale of Rephaim, the place was furtively referred to as the "Field of Blood." A potter's parcel. A field of agony and punishment with an insatiable thirst for blood.

At the high place of Tophet in the Valley of Hinnom parents once made their children pass through fire to appease the pagan god, Molech. The prophet Jeremias foretold that God would visit this awful wickedness with sore judgment, and would cause such a destruction of the people that the valley would become known as the Valley of Destruction.

Later, King Josias of Judah stopped the pagan sacrifices by deliberately defiling the high place, rendering it unfit even for idolatrous rites. Even so, from the horrors of its fires, from its pollution by Josias, and perhaps also because offal was burnt there, the valley became a type of sin and woe.

The Hebrew name for this place, *Geben-Hinnom*, was

eventually corrupted into *Gehenna*, and passed into use as a designation for the place of eternal punishment.

Today, just before the start of Passover, the withered vale coils in the brooding morning shadows, as if sampling the breeze with a forked tongue: *Geben-Hinnom. Gehenna. Akeldama. Field of blood.*

A viper awaiting its prey, the potter's field pauses, probing. It seems to quiver and sway knowingly: more blood is sure to come.

AKELDAMA

One

Meandering into the *suk*, Yo-hannah swatted an airborne net of gnats as she made her way to the silver seller's stall. Slim and supple, the olive-skinned young woman moved quickly and deliberately, seeking a special gift.

Ordinarily, Yo-hannah would have sent one of the lesser maidservants of Herod's household on such an errand, but this gift was for her husband's birthday and she decided to make the trip herself. Yo-hannah's smooth, slender fingers stroked the hems of lambskin cloaks at the weaver's stall en route to the silver seller, pausing long enough to trade village gossip.

A tangle of alleys filled with colorful wares, noise, bustle and flavors, the *suk* was the shopping center of town. Shops and work places opened directly onto the lanes by way of wide archways which were shuttered at night. Shopkeepers displayed their goods in the open while craftsmen worked on the street in front of their shops. Pungent garlic, cumin and dried fish fought for supremacy with the more gentle aromas of cinnamon, coriander and fresh mint sprigs in the stifling heat.

Energy dwindled during the intense summers that filled the Galilee basin. Heat rolled off the hills in waves, scorching the dry land in burnt umber and sienna. Everyone welcomed the mild winters when, for a few brief weeks, rain transformed the withered landscape with fresh greens, scarlet anemones and yellow mustard flowers. Even without a heat wave, however, there was never any rain in summer when life is sustained by dews and mists.

~

The ache in her joints was vociferous. *When was the last time I rose in the summer dawn to climb the hills above Nazareth? Or looked to Mount Carmel to see the plain below covered with low white clouds and waited for the surrounding mountains to emerge like islands?*

Old Hadessa knew well the night mist which forms in the summer because the Carmel range is so close to the sea. *As soon as the sun rises, the mist disappears.* Just like the Jewish hope of Mashiah, the promised deliverer for whom all Yisrael held her breath and placed her hope, waiting as a bride awaits her groom.

But Mashiah was as far away today as Mount Carmel and Hadessa had an empty market basket to fill. She hauled her ancient frame off her pallet, dressed hurriedly and lumbered through the doorway into the misty blue of morning. Her tired bones protested every step to the *suk*.

"And how is the steward of Herod these days, and his accounts?" Hadessa inquired of a camel driver who had stopped to water his caravan at the well near the fringe of the bazaar. A stout woman of ancient age, Hadessa was a cook from a Galilean villa whose keen eyes, quick hands and razor tongue yielded her the freshest produce, most succulent meat, the finest fish, and the best wine at bargain prices.

"Chuza will find no cause to complain with the profits from this trip," the camel driver grunted, slurping water from a leaky gourd. Hadessa nodded amiably and kept her own counsel almost as closely as she kept an eye on the steward of Herod the Tetrarch and the steward's wife.

In truth, the venerated ancient need not have undertaken the trek to the *suk* at all. The tedious trip could have easily been delegated to a younger servant of lesser rank and greater alacrity. But as one whose haggling expertise was legendary, Hadessa delighted in the diurnal trip and the newest opportunity to mingle with friends and neighbors as she sought to buy more for less.

"Besides," Hadessa smiled smugly to herself, "Chuza's birthday is next week. My lamb will no doubt seek his gift at the *suk* today or tomorrow, and no one can get a better deal for her at a better price than I!" Hadessa's thick lips parted in a toothy grin, her amber eyes gleamed at the thought of finding Chuza's wife at the *suk*. It had been more than a week since their last visit and she wanted recent news.

Hadessa was the most trusted friend of Yo-hannah's mother, Tirzah. Brash, brawny, and as good-hearted as she was boisterous, the portly Hadessa folded a protective wing over the young woman when the girl's mother died of the brain fever. Yo-hannah never knew her father and was barely four years old at her mother's death, fragile and helpless.

Hadessa had no family of her own. She was old when Tirzah extracted a deathbed promise from her, pledging lifelong care and protection of her only child. Thus, faithful old Hadessa knew where her life would lead.

Or so she thought.

Years later, it was Hadessa who stood next to the marriage canopy in the place reserved for Yo-hannah's mother. The old one beamed with joy as Yo-hannah and Chuza exchanged wedding vows. That was nine years ago.

A year after the wedding, it was Hadessa who came rushing to Yo-hannah's side as the young woman's frail body doubled over in labor pains; it was wise, faithful Hadessa who tenderly bathed, dressed and helped bury four stillborn babies in five years, one right after another.

It was Hadessa who stood by Yo-hannah's side when Rephaiah was born. The pregnancy had been difficult, the birth even worse. After delivery the mid-wife solemnly warned the new mother against having any more children. "You have never been strong," the mid-wife scolded, "but your health has deteriorated further and is now quite delicate."

Yo-hannah searched the mid-wife's face, uncertain as to her meaning. The old woman turned her back momentarily, putting away her cloths, potions and poultices. When the mid-wife turned to face Yo-hannah, her gray face was grave. "Having another baby will kill you."

Hadessa watched as the pronouncement hammered its meaning into Yo-hannah's mind like a death sentence. She saw the light in her lamb's eyes sputter and die like a lamp hid under a bushel.

What a difference four years and a bright-eyed little boy made.

Smiling at the *suk* this morning while little Rephaiah played at the home of a cousin, Yo-hannah spotted Hadessa at the other end of the street, near the potter's stall. Yo-hannah raised her hand in greeting and then froze.

No. Not again. Not now. Not here. The affliction was bad enough when it stalked her and pounced at home, behind the private walls of her own garden or chambers, but here in the pulverulent streets of a public marketplace? Yo-hannah knew the ravenous grip of the searing pain all too well, enough to know that resistance was futile. Her only hope was to reach the big, strong arms of Hadessa before the pain rendered her immobile.

Yo-hannah lunged toward Hadessa, who in turn raised her eyebrows, puzzled. One look at Yo-hannah's ashen face and Hadessa bellowed, "Out of the way!" She could move surprisingly fast for a woman of such bulk, but this was her Yo-hannah! Her lamb. Child of her dearest friend. Yo-hannah: *Yahweh is gracious.*

Yahweh may be gracious, but he has no arms to catch my lamb now! Hadessa charged through the crowded street like a ram to its rival. Shawls and cloaks went flying, potteries clattered to the ground. Piles of pomegranates were reduced to blood-red rubble; peddlers scurried out of the way as the gray-haired speedster shoved and pushed her way through the throng. Arms outstretched, the faithful friend reached Yo-hannah just as the young woman collapsed, motionless.

Two

The hubbub died down, the lights faded and darkness descended on the city. Gates groaned open and disgorged a long column of grim fugitives into the valley. A large retainer of soldiers and servants indicated that the stealthy escapees were no ordinary residents.

The cortege headed south across the hills toward Bethlehem, whose sparse, stony fields better suited for grazing flocks than for concealment. Their leader was a muscular, imposing man in his early thirties. Tossing surreptitious glances over his shoulder, he seemed to expect pursuers at any moment. Among the fugitives were his sister, his mother, and his intended bride, the beautiful Miriam. The women and children, tears streaming down their faces, turned their backs on their beloved Yerushalayim—for how long? No one could say.

The dusty band passed Bethlehem as the pale pre-dawn of morning robed the hills. An attack by roving Parthians was successfully repelled, as was an attempted ambush by a band of Jewish rebels. When the group reached Idumea their leader rested, for this was his native land. Then he held a council of war.

It was agreed that his closest family, guarded by the lightly armed troops, about eight hundred in all, should take refuge in the precipitous stronghold of Masada, an isolated, rocky fortress towering high above the western shore of the Dead Sea. Much of the surrounding land lies in the arid, barren Wilderness of Judea, which extends over the lower eastern terrace of the hill country. It is the retreat of hermits, robbers, and the politically persecuted. Life there was lonely, quiet, shadeless, hot, demanding, and reasonably safe.

Indeed, Masada was virtually impregnable. There were only two ways to the top of the wilderness fortress: a short one from the west side across a cliff face, and a torturously circuitous path up from the east. Well fortified and easily defended, the fortress had sufficient supplies of food and water to withstand a prolonged siege. The dark-bearded man secured his closest relatives in the wilderness stronghold and ordered the rest of his followers to disperse. Then he moved south.

Refused sanctuary by the Arabs, he made his way toward Egypt, where he was welcomed by the beautiful Cleopatra. The exotic queen received him with honor and arranged for him to be taken to Rome by sea. Over the next few years they were to become the bitterest of enemies. Had she known that her sudden guest was the future king of the Jews, Cleopatra may not have been so gracious a hostess. But she could not have realized that this breathless, dark-haired man with steady hands and iron will would one day be none other than Herod the Great, father of Herod Antipas, Tetrarch of Galilee and Perea.

Three

The most important river in Palestine, the Jordan flows north-south from Galilee, a territory in northern Palestine, through Samaria, past Jericho and Yerushalayim on the west and Perea to the east.

Jordan means "descender." Descend the river does, from sources near the mountains of Lebanon and Syria, including the snows of Mount Hermon. The river travels, often turbulently, to the Sea of Galilee. Leaving the Sea of Galilee at the sea's southern side, the Jordan flows first rapidly and then with diminishing speed down the sixty- five mile valley between the mountains of Samaria to the west and those of Gilead to the east. Here the Descender slices through a deep rift known as *El-Ghor,* through which the Jordan twists and turns like a serpent until it empties into the saline waters of the Dead Sea, the lowest point on the earth's surface.

Natural fords occur at the mouth of the river near Jericho. This is where people, animals, and goods can cross the hundred foot wide stream. Coming from Yerushalayim and Judea to the Jordan, people travel by way of the trade route running between Yerushalayim and Ammon. Near Jericho the Descender slows its rush by broadening out into shallow and quiet pools. Here the water is calm and safe enough for people to enter with ease, as some did in response to a camel hair-clothed, locust-eating, vociferous herald known as Yo-hannan the Baptizer.

As far as is known, the Jordan River stands alone among the rivers of the world in that the greater part of its course runs below sea level.

~

Fringed with thickets of tamarisks, oleander and soft arcs of graceful willows, each side of the ravine through which the river rushed was flushed with flowers. The beautiful setting was deceptive. Chava knew that lions often lurked in the dense shrubbery surrounding the water, and thus made haste to her southern destination.

Travelers walking the ancient road north from Yerushalayim to Samaria, after most of a day's journey, would note a striking change in the countryside. Behind lay the high tableland of Judea. Samaria lay in front, with its mountainous terrain cut by many deep, wide, and fertile valleys. Historically, the hill country of Judea was easily defended and seldom captured, while Samaria, with little natural defense, was regularly overrun by invaders.

Like her?

Returning from a visit north, Chava's eventual destination was the Holy City. But it was far to the south and she would stop first at Sychar, her home town. She would stay as long as it pleased her and then resume her pilgrimage south to the Holy City in time for Passover.

Sychar was a town of Samaria, in the vicinity of the land given by Ya'cov to his son Yosef, about half a mile from Ya'cov's well. Renowned for the sweetness of its water, the well is hand dug, stone-lined, and one of the deepest in Palestine, about two days' journey on the route between Yerushalayim and Samaria.

Independent and headstrong, the auburn-haired, pink-cheeked young woman began her journey south in the company of several families. She kept her own council and her identity a secret. Chava followed the troupe at a distance, reasoning that distant company was better than none. But the group turned east for Decapolis this morning and Chava found herself alone, wishing for a faster route. It was much quicker and easier to take the more direct path along the Jordan, but Chava knew that a westward hitch at Scythopolis was her only option. She would make the detour in a few miles.

For now, heat ricocheted off the river and swam in the dead air in desiccated ripples. Shadows shimmered along the water. Her sandals and garments coated with dust and grime, Chava allowed herself a brief rest along the river banks. Thirst clawed at her throat, but everyone from Galilee to Judea knew that this stretch of the Jordan was particularly treacherous. Swift currents frequently swept pilgrims away. Though her waterskin was almost empty, Chava could not swim and thus dared not chance the churning waters of the Jordan River, "the descender." Nursing a blistered heel, the Samaritan woman cursed her stupidity for choosing the smaller, lighter waterskin over the larger, heavier one.

Would that I could walk through this plain unimpeded. Chava caught herself and nearly laughed at her own foolishness. *A half-breed allowed the direct route to Yerushalayim? A half-Gentile granted safe passage through pure Jewish towns? When pigs fly,* she muttered, readjusting her *keffiyah* against the noon glare.

Chava considered Yerushalayim, the Holy City, and wondered again: *Are you a God of pure Jews only? Of whole people alone? What of us foreigners and half-breeds? Will you "invade" us as well?*

Four

"How long has she suffered these dreadful spells?" Hadessa demanded of Yo-hannah's husband, Chuza. The steward of Herod Antipas, Tetrarch of Galilee and Perea, Chuza was a fastidious, capable man. Highly efficient and organized, Chuza had a rapier wit and a shrewd, calculating mind to match. But he was not unkind.

Another doctor was called. The Greek hovered over Yo-hannah, lying as dull and lifeless on the pile of silk cushions as a fallen corpse. Hadessa had carried her home from the market, shielding Yo-hannah from prying eyes and wagging tongues in the folds of her tunic.

Chuza was worried. The fainting spells began nearly four years ago, shortly after Yo-hannah's delivery of her first healthy child, a boy. The dizziness and nausea had increased in frequency and duration as the child grew.

Rephaiah gains health and strength daily, while my wife's own life seems to ebb away into her son. Chuza grimaced, "Since just after Rephaiah was born."

"Why was I not told sooner?" Hadessa rasped, indignant.

Chuza, pained, tried to explain. "There's nothing you could have done. At first Yo-hannah just brushed off the fainting spells, saying she was overtired or some wine did not agree with her. She refused to summon a doctor and would not allow any physician I called to even breach the doorway. But now." the tall, thin steward's voice trailed off unevenly as he blinked back tears.

Nothing escaped the eagle eyes of old Hadessa. *Chuza is a tough bird. Shrewd, and as sharp as a Roman sword. He has to be to serve that old buzzard, Herod Antipas. Not much ruffles Chuza's feathers. If he's worried about Yo-hannah this much, then her affliction must be...?*

Hadessa decided then and there. She would no longer be a cook in a neighboring villa, but a full-time guardian of her charge. "Make ready the guest quarters" the old woman barked, "I will be moving in tonight..."

The Steward of Herod Antipas knew better than to argue.

Five

Bunched around the Jordan in various clusters and plains, Palestinian geography includes limestone hills to the east, Mount Meron to the northwest of Galilee, and chunky, imposing Mount Hermon with its ghostly white eminence to the east. The country gives way to desert in the south that is inhabited only by bedouin. West of the Jordan valley are the provinces of Galilee, Samaria, Judea and Idumea. To the east lie Gaulantis, the Decapolis and Perea. Each has its own governor, procurator, or tetrarch. All writhe under the hobnailed *caligae* boot of Rome.

~

Baritone laughter and soprano giggles curved over the green river water where two couples shared a picnic *prandium* around mid-day. Childhood friends from the village of Derbe in Roman Galatia, a town between Lystra and Tarsus, Gaius Sextus and Julius Quintus were as close as brothers, proudly serving the great army of Rome.

For now their principal base in Judea was in Caesarea. The city had been built by Herod the Great for the Romans, as there was a natural harbor south of Mount Carmel. Detachments of soldiers from Caesarea were normally on duty in Jerusalem, stationed at the Fortress Antonia. But both men were on leave, awaiting fresh orders.

Veteran noncommissioned officers, centurions proudly numbered themselves among the most effective in the Roman army, and for good reason. Centurions were the backbone of the Roman army, rising through the ranks to posts of command because of their character and battlefield bravery. Hard military men, they commanded a "century," a unit of about one hundred men.

Burly and robust, Gaius and Julius were seasoned veterans of Roman campaigns. Weathered by sun and wind, Gaius was a man younger than his rugged features suggested. His chin was square and deeply cleft. A small white scar serrated his right cheek—the result of a confrontation with a Parthian sword. Gaius would soon lead a garrison under Pontius Pilate, the fifth regional procurator of Judea. Procurator Pilate controlled the area formerly run by Archelaus, brother of Herod Antipas, but the cagey procurator, or governor, had no jurisdiction over Galilee and Perea, where Herod Antipas ruled as tetrarch.

Julius would soon receive orders to return to Rome as part of the Imperial Regiment. But for now, the two old friends traded reports and insults like old wives swapping gossip. They nattered about the latest antics of Herod Antipas, son of the brutal, ruthless Herod the Great. Though certainly less cruel and ferocious than his infamous father, Antipas was equally cunning in his boorish attempts to rule the "vast, wandering rabble" that peopled Galilee and Perea.

The men refilled their wine goblets as their wives lazed by the nearby river. Figs, grapes, apples and pears spilled over the grass around boiled eggs, tangy goat cheese and fresh mushrooms, radishes and stewed veal. It was a lovely day, and the soldiers' reminiscing turned to their service under Sosius, when their commander aided Herod as the latter struggled for control of Judea.

Gaius scanned the stern countryside, quickly assessing terrain, distances, sun and shadow, potential ambush sites. It was his habit of many years; the fact that Gaius was on leave at the moment did not break it. "A strange country with a strange history," he opined.

Julius nodded. "Remember the siege of Jerusalem?" he inquired rhetorically, stabbing a slice from the rounded bread loaf he had just cut in two.

AKELDAMA

Who could forget Jerusalem?

"No visitor seeing Jerusalem for the first time can be unimpressed by its visual splendor" Julius had pronounced, recalling how he drew in his horse's reins and literally sat up in his saddle as they neared the city for the first time. Gaius was skeptical until he saw it for himself.

The long, difficult ascent from Jericho to the Jewish "holy city" ended as he and his troops rounded the Mount of Olives and suddenly caught sight of a vista like few others in the world. Across the Kidron Valley, set among the surrounding hills, was Jerusalem, "the perfection of beauty." In the words of the lament of the Jewish prophet Jeremias, the city was "the joy of all the world." Even a crusty Roman centurion had to confess a certain degree of grudging admiration for such a place.

The view from the Mount of Olives was dominated by the city's gleaming, gold-embellished temple. According to these troublesome Jews, this "temple" was the site of their god's earthly dwelling place. It was where their god mediated his throne and raised up a people to perform rituals and ceremonies that would foreshadow the coming of some future "deliverer." The temple itself stood high above the "City of David," at the center of a gigantic white stone platform.

To the south of the temple sat the Lower City, a group of limestone houses, colored yellow-brown from years of sun and wind. Narrow, unpaved streets and houses sloped downward from here toward the Tyropean Valley, which ran through the center of Jerusalem.

Rising upward to the west was the Upper City, or *Zion*, where the white marble villas and palaces of the wealthy stood out like patches of snow. Two large arched passageways spanned the valley, crossing from the Upper City to the temple.

The Roman siege of Jerusalem under Sosius was magnificent, but could have but one outcome: Roman victory. This translated into triumph for Herod Antipas, a man both centurions disliked intensely but whom they stingily respected for his cat-like cunning and the swift, decisive manner in which Herod Antipas ruled his tetrarchy and displayed his unswerving loyalty to Rome. *If the world isn't Rome and Rome isn't the world, then what is either?*

During the siege of Jerusalem Julius' regiment attempted to storm the north wall of the city, which was protected by two walls. He led the initial assault against the outer wall while Gaius, in an attempt to collapse the Jewish defenses, directed the attempt to undermine a stretch of the wall and bring in Roman battering rams.

"The Jews fought well," Julius admitted, swashing down another cup of wine mixed with water and honey. He had been impressed with the defendants' grim determination. The defenders tried to fire the Roman siege engines and when they failed, the Jews broke into the mines and fought the Romans hand-to-hand underground. In the end, both soldiers agreed, "the Jews were no match for superior Roman training and technique." Even so, it took months for the Roman army to break through Jerusalem's outer wall.

Retreating to the inner wall, the Jews fought back heroically, holding out for another two weeks. Their doom was imminent, yet they fought. Once over this final barrier, Julius and his troops burst into the Lower City, cutting the city in half. Some defenders fled to the temple. Others took refuge in the upper city. Both the temple and Upper City were stormed. Roman and Herodian swords spared neither women, children, nor the elderly.

"A foolish fellow and a woman," Gaius chortled derisively now, recalling how Herod had begged Sosius to call off his troops in order to prevent the desecration of the temple and the complete destruction of the city. Herod managed to prevent the despoliation of the temple, shouting that he wanted to rule a kingdom, not a desert. Thus the Hasmonean dynasty ended, and Herod ascended a blood-stained throne.

Six

Gaius winced involuntarily, remembering while Julius snoozed. He recalled another "history lesson" of sorts, a strange conversation he had had with his former armor bearer.

The centurion bought Arieh, *the lion,* at a slave market. Emaciated, battered, and crusted with filth, the young man's deprivations could not completely diminish a broad, dignified face, distinguished black features and ebony eyes as sharp as a dagger. He appeared to be perhaps eighteen years old. Bound hand and foot with heavy, clanking chains, there was something noble about the Nubian's erect carriage and strong shoulders.

"Not even a donkey within my stable would be treated as these miserable slave traders have treated this wretch." Moments later Gaius placed three gold sesterces into the trader's grimy, predacious hand.

"Unshackle him," Gaius pointed to the boy. Gaius was a Roman and a pagan. As such, he was arrogant, ruthless and brutal when necessary; generous and munificent when allowed. *Besides*, he scowled, *I hate to see talent and ability wasted in anything—beast, battlefield, or men.*

"But sir, this boy is violent and vicious" the wiry trader carped. "We keep him shackled to control him. It's the only way!"

Gaius drew himself to his full height, beefy forearms and neck rippling in the sun. "Are you in the habit of questioning the orders of a centurion of Rome?" Brawny and biting as a death adder,

Gaius was a force to be reckoned with, even from a distance. Up close and personal, he was as formidable as a Roman phalanx.

The trader blanched, then scurried to the Nubian and unchained him. Gaius motioned to the boy to follow him to his house. The Nubian did so without a word. When they arrived Gaius closed the gate and explained, "Even though I have purchased you from these vile fellows, you must know that I keep no slaves."

The boy's eyes glittered, but Gaius detected neither malevolence nor peril. "However, it so happens that I am in need of an armor bearer. If you are as stalwart a fellow as I think you are, you may come with me and learn. If not, I will complete the necessary papers for your *liberti* and you will be free to make your own way in this world."

Arieh, a dark-skinned Nubian of considerable wit and keen intellect, had no wish to return to the jail from which he had been extricated for the slave block after being wrongly accused as a "dangerous foreigner with an evil eye."

Bathed, well-fed, cleanly clothed and kindly treated, the Nubian proved an eager student, well-schooled, quick-witted and reliable. The centurion was not surprised to learn that Arieh*, the lion*, was of royal lineage. All in all, Gaius was pleased with his purchase, but for one thing: the boy's earnest and incessant petitions to his Unknown God.

Gaius knew about the Unknown God. He once sacrificed to Him in a Greek temple. *Who is the God with no name? The Jews sacrifice to him and call him Lord. But he has no images of himself. Who can see this God, know him?*

"He has no name that anyone speaks," explained Arieh a few months later as he polished the centurion's *lorica segmentata*, bands of steel tied together with leather strips to protect the chest and belly, much like plates of armor protect a lobster. He next attended Gaius' helmet, which included cheek guards to protect the face, an extension at the back to protect the neck, and a reinforcing bar across the front to help save the skull from chopping blows from above. As he worked, Arieh insisted that this "unknown god" was intent on saving all men, regardless of position or person. "He is the God of the Jews, the God of all men."

"What?" Gaius sneered, voice as sharp as an unsheathed sword.

"Yes, God of the Greeks, Romans, Jews, slaves and free."

"How do you know this?" Gaius asked, incredulous. Gaius regarded their relationship as one of comrades more than as master and slave, although Arieh maintained a respectful deference at all times.

"I know from the writings of our holy book, and in my heart," the boy replied matter-of-factly as he moved on to check Gaius' *pilum*, his seven foot-long spear. Arieh then attended the centurion's double-edged *gladius*, and finally the shield. The *scutum* was nearly four feet high, three feet wide, rectangular in shape, and curved slightly outward so that legionaries could hide their bodies within the curvature. As was the custom, Gaius' shield was painted red with a golden lightning bolt.

Gaius decided to play along. It had been a slow, peaceful summer day. A crimson sunset haloed the palm fronds off the Mediterranean coast. The warm scent of lilac rose in the hot air. Gold and green globes hung like ponderous pendants on nearby fruit trees.

"Do you pray to this 'Unknown God'?" Arieh nodded.

"And what do you call him when you pray?"

The youth with sinewy shoulders didn't miss a beat, "I call him 'Father.'"

Gaius' brows furrowed and he took a step backward. "*Father?* No one calls any of the gods 'Father!'" *Outrageous! Preposterous! Absurd!*

But the armor-bearer was insistent. "The Unknown God smiles when one of his children calls him 'Father.' He loves his children."

Gaius froze in his tracks, jaw hitting the dust. *A "father" God who loves his children?? Ridiculous! Impossible! Inconceivable!*

Gaius threw back his head and laughed, "The gods don't love! They are conceited, powerful, petty, and malevolent, yes. Lustful, jealous, vengeful, capricious, of course. But *loving*?" Gaius snorted and ordered Arieh to take another draught of wine, thinking the seaside sun had addled the boy's brains. Stomping off, the centurion withdrew to his tent, thoroughly baffled for one who was rarely—if ever—baffled by anything. Or Anyone.

Seven

"Rephaiah?" Yo-hannah's voice edged higher, just a decibel or two short of panic. Recovered from yesterday's searing headache, another thought pressed on her brain. *Where is he?* She flew to the window and scanned the sun-splashed courtyard with a quick, practiced eye. No sign of the boy. Yo-hannah raced through their rooms, calling her son's name. *Maybe he's watching Salem shoe horses in the stable.*

She knew how much her son loved to watch the sleek, stately Arabians that populated King Herod's royal stables. And that Salem, the soft-spoken farrier, never wearied of explaining horses or horse shoes or nails to the insatiably curious boy.

"Rephaiah?" she shouted, bursting into the stable. Salem looked up from his anvil.

"My son?" she cried. "Is Rephaiah here?"

"No, lady," the old man replied as his eyes blazed, reacting to her alarm. The Lady Yo-hannah had always been kind to Salem, nursing him with broth and stuffed grape leaves when he'd been kicked by a horse. She baked him fresh bread and served up steaming spiced figs to help the old man regain his strength. She spoke softly to the farrier, according the old, nearly lame man a dignity and kindness that quenched his thirsty, lonely soul like an oasis in the desert.

More than that, Yo-hannah had secretly redeemed Salem's wife and only daughter, slaves of Herod's brother, Philip, at the cost of a priceless jade and pearl necklace and a fabulous ruby brooch. Salem could never prove it. No one could. It had all been done at arm's length, through a shadowy intermediary sworn to silence. The Lady Yo-hannah had never spoken of it herself, but Salem recalled the day the lady found him staring blankly into space above his fire, tears coursing down his hollow cheeks. She gently asked for an explanation as to the cause of his distress.

Soon thereafter it was rumored that an old woman from Galilee, a friend of Yo-hannah's mother, had made discreet inquiries concerning Salem's past. Someone had discovered the truth about the enslavement of his wife and daughter in the household of Philip, the ruthless and inept brother of Herod Antipas. It wasn't long afterwards that Shar'on and Ruth materialized on Salem's doorstep under cover of darkness, tattered and hungry, but free! *Liberti.* "Freedmen" by the initiative of another. The duo was redeemed, it was rumored, at an outrageous price from a silent benefactress who chose to remain anonymous.

"A fine wife and a fine seamstress, my rose," Salem mused quietly, eyes misting at the memory. Shar'on's exquisite handiwork in wool and linen had been considered and coveted as far away as Galatia. Taught on the loom at her mother's knee in Galilee, Shar'on wove on a large loom capable of producing a double width of material, wide enough for weaving the less commonly found and therefore more expensive seamless cloaks.

Some years ago a husky old woman purchased a prize homespun cloak from Shar'on's stall at the *suk*. Shar'on hesitated at first, assessing the graying hair and stooped shoulders with a practiced eye. But the old woman had surprised her by paying in silver shekels.

"A gift," the buyer beamed, "fit for royalty." Shar'on had seen neither buyer nor cloak nor recipient since. The sweetness of the memory brought tears to Salem's eyes. Even now, years after Shar'on had died and Ruth had married, he did not forget.

~

Salem bellowed an inquiry at one stable boy, then another, then at the boy who polished the bits and bridles. Salem organized a quick search of the stables. No one had seen Rephaiah all morning. Salem recalled the boy's penchant for water—river, spring or seashore--the boy loved water but could not swim.

A sense of dread crept into the farrier's old bones, followed by the steel wool of determination. If the lady's son was headed toward the sea, then Salem would hasten there as fast as his rickety old legs could take him.

Eight

Returned from the river, Gaius divested himself of wife and picnic companions and headed toward the nearest tavern, where he mulled over Julius' historical refresher like a crow with a bright bauble. In between munches of dates and dried fish he recalled the history lesson taught by his tutor when he was a young boy.

"You'd think that all their years of subjugation would have improved the Jews' behavior" the grizzled old man snorted, "but it hasn't."

It was true. During the six hundred years since Cyrus repatriated the Jews to Palestine, the quarrelsome people had been the sullen subjects of the Persian, Egyptian, Seleucid, and Roman Empires. The last few centuries were an unending ordeal to them because the Jews interpreted their repeated subjugations by foreign powers as evidence of their god's disapproval of them.

"Why don't they get a new god?" Gaius asked as a boy. Years later as a centurion, he wondered the same thing. There were certainly plenty to choose from within the pantheon of Roman deities. "If prayers, incense or offerings to one deity don't achieve the desired results, why not just move on to the next?"

Gaius entertained other thoughts that he dared not put into words, not even to his old friend and brother centurion, Julius. *Modern Rome,* he thought, morose. *The might of the world drowning in a cesspool of graft, corruption, greed and debauchery. The shining city peopled by soft, scheming senators, their conniving, depraved wives, and a fat, raptorial aristocracy whose indolent indulgences are paid for by crushing taxes extracted from worthier men. A shining city,* the centurion scoffed under his breath. *Shining city, indeed! More like a decadent bordello choking to death in its own dung.*

Yes, Rome. White and golden and insolent, the city sprawled on her seven hills, crowded against a cyan sky. The sun strummed the city walls like a nymph's fingers across lyre strings. Blood-red banners topped with furious gold eagles fringed the city gates.

Rome. Ferocious, depraved, swollen with people from many nations. The center of the Empire, with its regal hills, elaborate villas, its splendid aqueducts and magnificent archways. Licentious and lascivious, Rome embraced all the gods and religions of her conquered countries, stewed them into a seething cauldron of syncretism and served up a percolating pantheon of religions. Rome. Where divinity was displayed daily, but faith so hard to find.

Recently recalled from the Mediterranean coast to the choking, scheming seductress of the world, Gaius Sextus cursed as he re-read the scroll specifying his new orders.

"Palestine? Judea?" Gaius' face purpled with rage as he spat out the nouns like vomit. "That wretched patch of desert?" Certainly his battlefield boldness and loyal service to Rome deserved better than this! He eyed his armor and the harnesses atop it festooned with his *phalerae,* round disks signifying decorations for acts of bravery. But his orders had him posted to the end of the world.

Arieh shared his master's disgust and disappointment with this unexpected turn of events, but it was not his place to either reply nor question the orders of Tiberius. So he waited, allowing the fiery centurion to vent his wrath. Gaius' rage quelled eventually, and Arieh offered an observation. "Perhaps Caesar knows that the unruly rabble of Judea require a strong and decisive hand," he ventured, "the hand of a noble centurion." It was a feeble rejoinder, but the best that the young armor bearer could find at the time.

Sunset sprouted in Gauis' onyx eyes. "Does your 'god of love' have a hand in this? Can he give meaning to this outrage?"

Arieh bowed but remained silent. Gaius called loudly for another goblet of wine, burying his thoughts further in the handsome cup. He knocked over a salt container and quickly threw a pinch over his shoulder to ward off any ill omens or evil eyes that might be lurking about. As all Romans, Gaius was superstitious, and one could never be too wary when the capriciousness of the gods came into play.

"Master," Arieh purled at his elbow, "man gains meaning in knowing the Unknowable." Gaius shot him a stony glance. "God can be comprehended only by the spirit."

Gaius cuffed the boy, dismissed him, and turned ever more sullen.

Nine

Miles away and a few months later, another history lesson was in progress.

"Galilee and Perea together are not large enough to be called a kingdom," Salem lectured his stable boys, "but within them Herod Antipas possesses all the powers of a monarch."

"Is that why everyone calls him 'King Herod'?"

"It is indeed," Salem nodded. "Do not forget that while Herod Antipas may not be a 'king' technically, he inherited more of his father's cunning and less of the old king's ferocity than Archelaus did."

The boys shuddered.

"Herod was careful not to invite hostility to himself as did his brother. Yet the unrest in Galilee parallels that in Judea. Herod Antipas represents Roman rule. Remember what happened with the revolt against Archelaus?"

All the boys knew the history. When a revolt against Archelaus was in full swing in Yerushalayim, a violent uprising against the joint rule of Herod and Rome fanned to fever pitch in Galilee. It was occasioned by a general census taken for tax purposes. That revolt was led by a Zealot from the city of Gamala, Judah of Galilee.

Known as "Galilee of the Gentiles" or "Galilee of the nations" due to its diverse population, the region in northern Palestine is largely fertile and well-watered, with mountains in the north and southeast. Galilee became the center of a flourishing agricultural economy. Important trade routes intersected the area which often saw Romans and travelers from distant lands. As a result, Galilean Jews were more exposed to other cultures and value, which may have led to closer relationships with Gentiles than those had by the strict, "pure" Jews of Judea. Some "pure" Jews vilified Galileans for having diluted their faith for the sake of peace with their neighbors or brimming coffers. Hence, it was no accident that Judah came from Galilee, a hot bed of this brand of fiery Jewish nationalism.

"Was this a reaction of some to what they saw as the worldliness of their fellow Jews in Galilee?" Salem asked rhetorically. The boys shrugged, tearing off pieces of broiled chicken and chewing hard.

"Whatever the case, Judah called upon Jews of Galilee to make rebellion the sign of their commitment to God. He was hailed by many Galileans as a Mashiah who would deliver them from foreign bondage. Many joined him." Salem shook his head, shoulders sagging. He gulped down a half cup of wine, wiped his mouth with the back of his hand, and continued.

"Judah led a great mob of followers up to Sepphoris, where the people joyfully threw its gates open to him. He equipped all his followers with weapons from military stores they found in the armory of Herod Antipas. The rebels improved the defenses of the city, and Judah led his men in prayers to God to preserve them and the city during the Roman siege that was sure to ensue."

"What did Herod do?"

"Herod Antipas sent an appeal to Varus, that vile Roman, to put down the insurrection. The Romans laid siege to Sepphoris, then slaughtered the rebel garrison and destroyed the city. Varus did that in retribution for the support given to Judah by its inhabitants, whom he forced to dismantle all of its great buildings, leaving not one stone upon another."

"Widows can still be heard chanting prayers for husbands who joined Judah and were put to the sword in Sepphoris after it fell. So you can see why Galilee and Nazareth lack a good name throughout

Palestine."

Chewing slowed. Heads bobbed.

"But one thing stands in Nazareth's favor. The town is a local gathering point for the priests who meet to travel to Yerushalayim for their biannual duties in the temple. And of course we still hope for Mashiah, for divine deliverance from Roman rule."

"And this Mashiah, will he come?" Jethro asked, stretching and yawning to indicate a readiness for rest.

Salem's voice softened. He turned his aged head toward Yerushalayim. "Oh yes, boy. Mashiah will most certainly come. Perhaps in your lifetime, and if *El Elyon*, God Most High, wills," his eyes glistened like morning dew, "perhaps in mine."

Ten

Chava knew the story well.

Samaria was inhabited by a population of mixed ancestry. When the northern kingdom of Yisrael fell to the Assyrians, the victors deported large number of Yisraelites to Assyria, and had not her ancestors replaced them as settlers? Over time, her ancestors mixed with those of Jewish blood, and Jewish worship was affected. Her ancestors were half Gentile by descent, retaining some features of heathen worship, but they had Moishe's law and worshipped the One God of Yisrael, did they not?

"Schismatic, heathen!" the pure Jews spat, refusing to travel the direct route between Judea and Galilee, preferring instead to cross the Jordan and tread the roads on the river's eastern bank so as to avoid contamination through contact with the syncretistic half-breeds. Taunts darted through the air like dragonflies. *Jews do not associate with the Samaritans.*

Chava shrugged. *I guess nothing ever changes. Once rejected, always rejected. If I could just get to Yerushalayim, maybe I could know what it is to be a whole Jew, to be pure and accepted! Perhaps I can find Mashiah in the Holy City. If he would be anywhere, he would be there.*

Yerushalayim. Sacred city and capital of Judah, of Judea, of Palestine, and of Jews throughout the world. The royal city, the mountain of the Lord. *City of David. City of God. City of Zion.*

City of Peace.

Samaria. Founded when the ten northern tribes of Yisrael refused to acknowledge Rehoboam, the son of Solomon, as their king. Samaria. A dead-end on the road to Nowhere. A region whose name was synonymous with contempt, disdain, corruption.

Two cities, two temples. Two people groups. One bitter divide.

~

Chava bit her lip as a vanilla sky boiled clouds like chamomile tea. Her bold, thirsty eyes embodied a melancholy intelligence brimming with many thoughts, but it had been a long time since those thoughts focused on God or His holy city. Perhaps the pain of isolation and the craving of her insatiable heart had awakened in her a hunger for wholeness. *Yerushalayim*: City of Hope?

Are you there, Promised One? Do You hear? What would my life be if not for the mixed blood in my veins? If I was a whole Jew, a pure Jew? Part of a community rather than an outcast, a reject?

Pale and brittle, the cerulean sky pursed its lips in mute reply. There was no other.

Chava stood, slung her waterskin over a grimy arm and trudged determinedly south to her first destination: a house and a man. Both were squarish and "flat-roofed." Neither was hers.

AKELDAMA

Eleven

It was coming. Sudden and unpredictable, Yo-hannah knew the crippling headaches could strike at any moment, often without warning. But after so many she learned that the taste of camel dung in her mouth accompanied by a blacksmith pounding in her ears would not go away and could not be ignored. In a matter of moments the pain would blow through her head, pulverize her brain and scream into her blood.

The pain struck like a *khamsin*, the deadly desert wind which sucks strength from a man's limbs, fills the sky with a thick gray and strips the fields naked. So struck, Yo-hannah would crumple into a heap, inert, at the mercy of whoever happened along.

The wife of Chuza, steward of Herod Antipas, tried to ignore the migraines at first. But they had ballooned in frequency and intensity over the last few months, crushing her underfoot like a stampede of Hannibal's elephants. She felt healthy and strong for days—often weeks—between attacks. But sooner or later, Yo-hannah knew, she would see shimmering lights or blind spots, followed by nausea, vomiting, and an extreme sensitivity to light. Then the pain starting on the left side of her head would rip through her skull like a scavenging jackal and pound her sentience into powder. As surely as a Carthaginian crossing over the Alps, the pachyderm of pulverizing pain would invade Yo-hannah's head and trample her underfoot for another day. Or more.

When it did, she could barely perform her duties. Simple tasks such as bathing little Rephaiah, kneading bread or pouring wine became impossible when the beast struck, sinking its shrieking fangs deep inside her skull. After four years, the headaches now plunged her into a death-like coma lasting one to three days.

Not now. Not again. Not here. She was rushing to rescue her son. Her only son. Blind spots sprouted in front of her eyes, stars spotted her vision. Yo-hannah's limbs were as heavy as Salem's anvil, and nearly as lifeless. In a moment her head would seem to explode, her mind melt. She collapsed to her knees.

Word came from the servant's quarters earlier: "The teacher, the young carpenter from Nazareth, set up camp by the sea this morning. You know how much he loves the little ones. Carries them on his back, skips stones across the river with them. Tells them stories. Rephaiah knows all about the teacher. We were talking about him just last night, saying that Yeshua was coming today!"

No! Yo-hannah screamed silently. *Not Rephaiah. Not near the sea!*

Just two months previously the boy had wandered toward a stream lacing the Herodian fig orchards and vineyards, where Yo-hannah had taken him to join some cousins for a picnic. In the midst of setting out lunch—heaping dishes of couscous, raisins, peaches, steaming lentil stew and cool green cucumbers—Yo-hannah sensed an uneasy quiet. Turning suddenly, she rounded a trellis just in time to see Rephaiah swirling the stream with a stick some fifty feet away.

It was late summer. Storm clouds funneled over the land, discoloring the delicate crane's bill florets that dye the ground pink. Yellow mustard flowers cowered under the boiling clouds. Wild scarlet anemones rollicked near slim streams and parched springs. Heavy rain fell in the hills above, sending sudden torrents of water cascading down the dry, stony valley. The flash flood came without warning, washing away top spoil, displacing boulders, sweeping away shepherds with their flocks.

"Rephaiah! Come to Mother! NOW!" The thunder tore her voice from her throat, muted her shout to a whisper. The boy turned, caught his foot in a willow root, and fell face-first into the water. What had been a slim, shallow stream moments earlier was now a raging torrent. The stream did not yet run swift, but it was deep at this point, where Herod's gardener siphoned off water for the grape vines and fig trees.

Yo-hannah sped to the stream and plunged in after her boy. Drawing the unconscious child out of the murky water, she laid Rephaiah on the ground. She tried to expel the water in his lungs, slapping his back, willing him to breathe.

Please, Yahweh. Please! You have taken all the others. Four little boys, dead before they drew breath. Please leave me this little one!

Yahweh. "I am that I AM." Yahweh. The Name used of no one but Yisrael's God. Unchangeable in His relation to His people. Exclusive in character, being, person. Yahweh? Uncaused, uncreated, unchanging. Everlasting. Beginningless, endless. The One who is. The One who causes. Yahweh. *You told us Your name, too holy to be spoken by human lips.*

No response. Yo-hannah turned the boy over on his back, working his legs like a bellows. *Merciful One, please spare him! Yes, my ancestors failed to tear down the idols, to stop the child sacrifices to Molech. But let their sin be credited to my account, not my son's! He is my* only *son!*

Yahweh. *You are what You are, what You have always been and always will be*. Immutable. Changeless. Faithful. *You told us Your name, how You must long to be close to us. Be close to me now, be close to my son!*

"He's alive! He lives!" she announced moments later to the crowd that trailed her from the grape grove at the commotion. Yo-hannah clapped her hands in praise and thanksgiving as Rephaiah sputtered, spit up water and coughed. The experience had shaken her, and that night's wailing wind did not lessen the chilly memory.

That was two months ago. It was now September, Tishri, the start of the High Holy Days. She and Chuza and the boy were taking a few days' repose near the sea before undertaking the dull, dusty journey south to Yerushalayim for Passover. But where was Rephaiah today? Yeshua's camp wasn't close, but it could be close enough for a determined little boy. Yo-hannah's mother-mind closed on the camp's close proximity to the sea. She began to run, stumbling.

Twelve

A ragged band of followers ringed the son of Zebedee as he eased his small burden onto the shore. The fisherman was casting his hemp nets for morning fish when he noticed a small boy playing in the water.

Don't recognize that young lad; Yames' eyes followed the boy's antics as the four year-old splashed and kicked, watching soft arcs of silver glisten in the early sun. Coy, the sea billowed breathlessly under a cobalt blue sky. *Rather young to be so near the water alone.* Yames scanned the shore in search of a parent, aunt, sibling or servant. Black and white gull flashes speared the sunshine, jabbering. *I wonder if he knows about the thirty-foot drop-off just ahead...*

A moment later the boy's head bobbed, wild-eyed, and then submerged beneath the water. Yames waited, expecting the child's soft, olive-skinned face to crease the surface at any minute. It didn't. He waited another moment and then the fisherman plunged into the water without drawing in his seine.

Yames was swift with hand nets and none could draw in a catch of perch or carp faster, but his skill was fishing, not swimming. By the time Yames reached the spot where Rephaiah went under, the fisherman dove twice and came up empty. Another frantic dive and Yames' groping, callused fingers closed around the boy's left arm. It was already limp. The sea creamed calmly against the sand as

Yames pulled the boy to the surface and rushed him to the beach. Was he too late?

Thirteen

"What events caused me to come to this, a refugee to Rome?" Herod mused as he sailed toward Caesar. Nearly three centuries before, Alexander conquered the vast Persian Empire of which Yerushalayim had been a part. After Alexander's death the empire was sliced up and served to his three generals. The eastern end of the Great Sea became the kingdoms of Egypt and Syria. Judea, the home of the Jews, belonged to Egypt but was claimed by Syria.

Gaius mused over the same history. He knew that the people of Judea lived on a small, high, almost physically barren plateau. *Geography gives them a strong defensive position with natural barriers on all sides: the Jordan Valley to the east; the Negev Desert to the south; the steep inclines rising from the maritime plain to the west; the deep ravines along the border with Samaria to the north.* He turned the terrain over and over in his military mind. *This awkward little hill country is the homeland of a 'people chosen of god?'* The centurion snorted. It didn't make sense any more than their history.

More than a hundred years before Herod's birth, Judea came under Syria's control. The Syrian King Antiochus IV decided to reorganize his domain to give it the benefits of Greek thought and civilization. He thought to force this "benefit" upon the Jews. When he insisted that they change their religious practice to include the worship of false gods and graven images, the Jews rebelled under the Maccabean brothers.

The Syrians tried to quell the rebellion but failed. Thus, Judea became virtually independent and was ruled by the Maccabean family, the Hasmoneans. The Hasmoneans became the high priests and the governors of the country. To keep Syria in check the Hasmoneans made treaties with the new superpower that was Rome.

The Judean state grew in strength and stature in the next fifty years, conquering and capturing the surrounding lands of Samaria and Galilee in the north and Idumea and Perea in the south and east. All were forced to adopt the Jewish religion. Herod was an Idumean. It was during this period that the Jewish religion split into two opposing groups – the Pharisees and the Sadducees.

"So, these religious lawyers, who are they?" Gaius asked Julius a fortnight ago. He usually left the cleaning and polishing of his armor to his servant, but his *machaira*, his short killing sword, was a matter he attended to personally. Gaius did so now as he pumped his old friend for information about his new post. Julius had already served two years in the god-forsaken Judean hills. He was more than eager to head for Rome and the Imperial Regiment, even if it meant parting with his best friend yet again.

Gaius held up his dagger and frowned, dissatisfied. The remainder of his weapons—a double-edged sword of about twenty-three inches, a javelin of a little over six and a half feet with an iron head and a sharp point to pierce shields and a barb to prevent its removal—already gleamed in the corner. Gaius bent over his short blade, wishing he hadn't been so amiable in freeing Arieh when the youth expressed his desire to return home to his own people.

I wonder if Arieh's "Father God" heard the boy call upon Him for guidance as he journeyed home to an uncertain fate? And if He heard, did He answer? Gaius frowned further. He scoffed at the idea of a "merciful" god who listened to anyone on *any* subject. Gaius' thoughts roamed as he alternately worked a rubbing cloth and a whetstone.

Julius continued. "The Sadducees control the high priesthood and hold the majority of the seats in their Sanhedrin. They may be exacting in Levitical purity, but they also attribute everything to free will."

"And their attitude towards Rome?"

"Sadducees are an aristocratic, politically minded group willing to compromise with Rome. You'll have little trouble from them," Julius crossed his beefy arms. "They'll side with Herod Antipas and Rome in the case of any religious controversy or rebellion. These Sadducees may be a conquered people," he cracked his knuckles, "but they know on which side their bread is buttered."

"And the religious lawyers, the Pharisees?" Gaius worried some more over his blade. He nicked his thumb and swore, cursing the loss of his faithful, if not fanciful armor-bearer.

"The name 'Pharisee' comes from the Jewish word for 'separated,' because they separate themselves from those who are not also Pharisees. Their roots go back some two hundred years to the Hasidim."

"Hasidim?"

"Pious Jews who joined forces with the Maccabees during a Jewish revolt against the Syrians. Now known as Pharisees, these men are strict in their observance of Jewish law, precise in its interpretation." Julius paused. Both he and Gaius could appreciate strict interpretations of the law, especially Roman law.

"Furthermore, these Pharisees believe in a continuing development in the understanding of the law. New interpretations become binding for them by approval of an assembly of accredited rabbis. The result is that Jewish religious law has become more and more complex. Isn't it true that any code of laws which can be amended by lawyers will in time become so complicated that no one but lawyers will understand it?"

Gaius shifted and tossed Julius a mocking grin, "Surely, and even they will disagree. But it seems like a lot of work for a feeble return. What kind of commands do these 'separated ones' keep?"

"Many of their commands surround their holy days, festivals and their day of rest, which they call a 'Sabbath' or 'Shabbat.' Regarding Sabbath observance, the command against work on the Sabbath was given in the context of the building of the Tabernacle. But their Oral Law defines work according to every process involved in making the Tabernacle."

"Such as...?"

"Such as a list of thirty-nine types of agricultural work—you know, work with skins, cloth, metal, wood and so on."

"I'm a soldier, not a farmer or a carpenter," Gaius replied, rolling his blunt, dark eyes.

Julius replied in mock irritation, "Do you want to learn about the people you will keep in line here, or not?"

"Alright, alright. So, thirty-nine types of farming work..."

"Yes, and each category is subdivided into thirty-nine more activities, making more than one thousand, five hundred and twenty one in all. None of these can be performed on the Jewish Sabbath, including dragging an object across an earth floor."

"What?"

"Their Pharisees consider *that* 'plowing,' which is prohibited work on their day of rest."

Gaius rolled his eyes. "What else?"

"They determine how far a person can walk -- a Sabbath day's journey."

"How far is that?"

"Two thousand paces," Julius fought a losing battle to retain his composure as Gaius' eyebrows shot skyward. "If a house falls on someone on the Sabbath, he should be left inside—if he lives. It would be breaking the Sabbath to pull him out! And plucking a few ears of corn and rubbing the husks away? Why, that's reaping and winnowing! Forbidden on their Sabbath. Hundreds like that."

"So, this 'Yeshua' we've been hearing about, the wonder-worker from Galilee. He seems to be no friend of these Pharisees, yet they share the same god? Why the conflict?"

"Partly because the Galilean is so popular with the common people, with whom the 'Separatists' have made such little headway." Julius rubbed his clean-shaven, cleft chin. "But it seems to me, brother centurion, that the crux of the matter seems to be that in seeking to live according to their law, these 'Separatists' have perhaps failed to understand what their law is about. No one points this out more succinctly than this Yeshua fellow."

A kernel of truth floated in Julius' statement. Gaius sensed it, hidden like a pearl in an oyster. But he had little patience for riddles or enigmas. "Has a tongue as sharp as my *gladius*, does he?" Gaius motioned to his recently whetted Roman stabbing weapon. Twenty-two inches long and three pounds in weight, the *gladius* was used for close work. *Kill a man with that and I can smell his sweat.*

Julius shook his head. "That's the thing about this Galilean. The common people love him for his kindness and compassion. He seems to reserve his sharpest stabs for their religious leaders."

"Why is that?"

"Perhaps you can tell me, brother centurion."

"I can't say that I can," Gaius remarked as he stood and stretched. "It's no small wonder that the people this Yeshua seems so fond of have been ground underfoot by one conqueror after another. They're so busy defending their laws, when can they defend themselves? How can anyone keep track of one thousand, five hundred and twenty… what was that?"

He recalled something Arieh, his young armor bearer once said, "God cannot be understood, cannot be discerned, coded or decoded. Those who wish to know him must come to him by faith."

"One thousand, five hundred and twenty one," Julius returned, swatting a buzzing horsefly. "And those are just the commands surrounding the Sabbath. Few people can cope with such a scrupulous adherence to the law other than the Pharisees themselves, who in turn see the people as 'sinners.' Pharisees wouldn't touch a non-Pharisee with a barge pole. In fact, Pharisees call non-Pharisees the *am ha' aretz*, 'people of the land.' You know, peasants, or more pejoratively, boors."

"The Pharisees also believe in the resurrection of the dead, in the immortality of the soul, and in reward and retribution after death. They fancy themselves champions of human equality and emphasize ethical teaching over theology." What the otherwise well-versed Roman did not yet know was that according to the Pharisees, God's grace extended only to those who kept His law.

"*They* call these peasants 'boors'?" Gaius slapped his thigh.

He couldn't help it. Peals of mirth plastered the room as both centurions exploded into laughter.

Fourteen

Veronica pushed back the blanket and crept out of her bed. Outside, the sky blushed coral as the village awakened with its usual cacophony: a rooster's lusty crowing, yapping dogs, fat brown donkeys braying in protest against their loads of figs, balsa or melons. The breeze fingered the curtain on her window and dropped it listlessly. Not yet mid-morning and the air outside was already torrid and twisting.

Blessed art Thou, Yahweh tsebhaoth, King of Glory who is surrounded by angelic hosts, who rules heaven and earth in the interest of Your people, and who receives glory from Your creatures.

King of *what?*

The outside air seeped into Veronica's Capernaum estate as despair slithered around her heart and squeezed. The widow of a wealthy vintner, Veronica slid out of her single bed and held out a trembling hand against the rough limestone wall, steadying herself against the swoon she knew would follow. It always did.

Staring at the puddle of red that stained her sheets again, Veronica coughed feebly into her omnipresent handkerchief. She knew that a quick vertical rise meant a sudden faint as her already low blood pressure plunged to subterranean depths with the effort to stand. So she learned to move slowly, deliberately and carefully, hoping to cheat the incessant flow out of a few drops of her life.

But she was worsening. Her condition deteriorated with each passing day.

~

Dimitri frowned. He was the latest in a long line of perplexed physicians. Clean-shaven and tanned, the young doctor reiterated the phrase Veronica had come to loathe, "I'm not sure... it may be... can't be certain..." Shrugging his shoulders, the Greek finally admitted, "I can't help you. No one can. But here," he handed her a small violet vial, "Take two drops of this twice a day. It won't stop the bleeding, but it will make you more comfortable."

More comfortable? She wanted to scream. *How can isolation and despair be made "more comfortable?"*

Veronica's maidservant ushered the doctor out of the hall and into the open courtyard. Listless, Veronica stared at the vile-smelling vial. She slowly deposited it on her dressing table where it joined a menagerie of similar vials, boxes, lotions, amulets and potions. All equally ineffective to halt the flow that no one could explain nor cure.

Worse than her physical malady was Veronica's social status. Ceremonially "unclean" because of her condition, Veronica was barred from participating in temple rituals and lived in virtual isolation but for her servants. Worse yet were the whispers. Some guessed at her condition, others assumed.

... Killed her husband in his sleep, I heard.

... Let's not forget that dashing Gallo-Roman officer awhile back, and she such a pretty young lass to be married to old Yitzhak.

... Always wondered about Yitzhak's sudden demise... plump and merry one day, stone cold dead the next.

... Poisoned his lentil stew, I hear. Blamed him for the loss of their boy..

... Didn't she have another husband, Zaccheus of Yerushalayim? Heard he went off to be a hermit.

... A tragedy that young Ya'cov got in over his head, but Yitzhak couldn't swim either, could he?

... Niece of Herod the Great, that's what they say. Can you imagine, here in our own town of Capernaum! Or was that grand-niece?

... Yes, a princess of Edessa.

... Cursed. A divine judgment, this illness. Retribution for some terrible sin.

... She's the daughter of the woman of Canaan. Yes, the Greek, born in Syrian Phoenicia. Imagine a pagan like that trying to get the attention of a rabbi.

Veronica heard it all. The furtive whispers, sentential stares. Prickly silences. How could she defend herself against a malady neither she nor any physician could understand or treat? The hemorrhage had made her ceremonially unclean for a dozen years, just after she lost her beloved Yitzhak.

Today she heard something else.

Snippets of astonishment floated through her window, stories from last week about a carpenter from Nazareth. Stories drenched with lovingkindness, dripping with mercy, revival, healing, freeing, faithfulness—could they be true? Could *he* be true?

Fluttering like a young butterfly under a noon day sun, something stirred in the ill woman's soul.

Fifteen

When it came to dabbling in eastern affairs to suit her wants and wishes, Rome was neither stranger nor amateur. In fact, Rome had amused herself with entrées into eastern affairs for more than a hundred years before Herod's flight from Jerusalem, setting up and toppling kings as she saw fit. In 67 B.C. Pompey, the greatest Roman general of his day, thrust eastwards crushing all before him. He advanced as far as the Caspian Sea and then turned southwest into Syria which was in a state of anarchy.

The brothers Hyrcanus and Aristobulus, rivals for the Hasmonean lands, both sought Pompey's help. The Roman sided with Hyrcanus, the weaker of the two, and the easier to control. Bitterly disappointed, Aristobulus seized Jerusalem. Pompey advanced on the city and Aristobulus retreated to the temple, which was built like a fortress. It fell after a three-month siege.

Pompey had heard a great deal about this temple which only priests were allowed to enter. His curiosity got the better of him and he and his staff went into the temple and entered the Holy of Holies which the Jews believed was the throne room of God. The Romans touched nothing, but the Jews never forgave Pompey, nor forgot his sacrilege.

Once again the Jews lost their liberty. The empire of the Hasmoneans was dissolved and divided. Sour, brutish Hyrcanus was allowed to rule Samaria and the coastal strip, a much-reduced realm. Judea became a puppet whose strings were pulled by Rome.

Well-known as "stubborn and stiff-necked," the Jewish people rejected Roman settlement and took to arms a few years later. Hyrcanus put down the revolt with help from Gabinius, the Governor of Syria. After crushing the revolt, Hyrcanus divided the Jewish state into five self-governing districts. He remained in Yerushalayim, a bitter figurehead lacking any real power. That now rested in the hands of his chief minister, Antipater. Herod's father.

"My only hope of keeping command is continued favor from Rome," Antipater realized, knowing this would be easier said than done. War clouds gathered. Currying Rome's favor and might would not be easy. The new Parthian empire threatened in the east and Rome herself seemed bound for civil war.

The Roman Empire was controlled by three men at this time: Pompey, Crassus, and Julius Caesar. Each swore to help the other two. Caesar acquired the provinces of northern Italy and swept toward Gaul. Pompey had Spain. Avaricious, pompous Crassus governed Syria.

Fancying himself a new Alexander, Crassus set out on world domination. Before doing so, he plundered the treasure of the temple in Yerushalayim and the Jews considered it divine retribution when both Crassus and his army were destroyed by the Parthians.

After Crassus' death, Pompey and Caesar realized that the world was not big enough for both of them. Caesar seized Italy; Pompey retreated east. Caesar followed and defeated Pompey decisively. The beleaguered old general fled to Egypt, where he was assassinated.

In the closing stages of Rome's civil war, Herod's father, Antipater, supported Julius Caesar. In gratitude Caesar restored his master, Hyrcanus, to his position as ruler of the Jews. Antipater himself was given the official title of Procurator of Judea. Herod, about twenty five years old, was given command over Galilee.

Sixteen

Nazareth, in lower Galilee where Yeshua grew up, sits on a summit at six hundred feet above sea level within the ancient tribal territory of Zebulun. The village is located in an amphitheater of arid hills just to the north of the Valley of Esdraelon, where the wood-scrubbed knolls of Naphtali rim the distance. The narrow pavement of the Via Maris runs through that valley on its way from Egypt to Syria, Parthia, and Babylon. Swaying caravans of camels carry the wealth of nations over that straight highway. Nazareth was thus a rural town deemed so infinitesimal and insignificant that it does not merit a mention in the Talmud's list of villages in Galilee. But the Sea of Galilee is another matter.

Sea birds, larks and finches swoop over the streams of Kishon en route to the thirteen-mile long, seven mile wide Sea of Galilee, also called the Sea of Gennesaret. The sea lies in a geological depression formed by the steep hills of Gilead to the east and the equally steep hills of Galilee to the west. Within the narrow confines of this small valley the days are short. Sunrise trims the eastern heights late. Twilight settles as soon as the afternoon sun is obscured by the rim of the western hills.

Pocketed in these heavily wooded hills, the sea is also subject to sudden, teeth-rattling storms. In winter, hot dry windstorms blow with destructive force from the eastern desert. In summer, cool air borne by westerly winds sweeps down the treeless slopes and strikes the hot, humid air that accumulates over its surface, resulting in vociferous tempests.

The Sea's shoreline bustles with agriculture, fruit growing and fishing. The Sea's waters abound in fisherman and fish, which are exported throughout the Roman Empire. Sepphoris, the largest city in Galilee, clacks its bustling tongue a few miles to the north.

An almost unbroken line of buildings and cities dot the Sea's shores: Capernaum and Bethsaida to the north, Kerza to the east, and further west and south lie Cana, Nazareth, and Nain. To the west sprawl Magdala and Tiberias, site of Herod's huge palace and home to Salem, his mistress Yo-hannah and her family.

Salem savored his location close to the shores of "harp lake." Any quiet place on the Sea of Galilee's west bank was cool, green, teeming with life—as many as forty different types of fish! The western shores were lapped by water pure enough to drink. He loved watching dawn break over the mountains of Gilead and morning light pour over the water and spread across the whole sea like melted butter. Salem inhaled contentedly. He loved the way the sweet spring breeze sang through the olive trees, or ruffled his eave with a cool hand on an otherwise sweltering night. But with his mistress' child unable to swim and so close to the water, now Salem wasn't so sure about the sea.

"Well, there are plenty of extra eyes and ears for the little one" Salem reasoned. "How can one small boy get into any watery trouble with so many intent upon his welfare?" Salem mopped his wrinkled brow and shook the nagging worries aside even as he headed toward the seashore.

Early yesterday Salem heated iron to a red glow in a forge, which a boy kept hot by hand-operated bellows. Then Salem meticulously transformed the red-hot metal into three hinges, four latches, two andirons, and no less than eight perfect shoes to protect the tender feet of his master's matched pair of splendid gray Arabians.

The old man wiped his hands on his leather apron as evening beckoned over the hills. A quintet of former street urchins and orphans-turned stable boys surrounded him like students around their rabbi.

"A little food, boys," senescent Salem grinned kindly yesterday, "history always tastes better on a full stomach." To the delight of his farrier protégées, Salem produced fresh dates and kumquats, pitas filled with strong goat cheese, honey oat cakes and for a special treat because all had labored so hard and so well this day—dried apricots and almonds. A fistful for each boy.

The youngsters trickled in to the villa one by one, from different parts of the countryside. Some boys were abandoned, others orphaned. Some still bore the scars and scabs of adult anger. His Shar'on could never turn away a hungry mouth nor shoo away a shivering shoulder. The Lady Yo-hannah had somehow found work for each ragamuffin under the wise and patient tutelage of old Salem, who treasured each mischievous, light-eyed imp like he was his own.

"Now, where were we?" Salem began, settling his tired old bones onto the stump of a fig tree almost as ancient as he. He had spoken of Herod the Great the day before, explaining that as unpopular as Herod the Great had been, his death came as a blow to the people of Nazareth just as it did to Jews everywhere.

"Ah yes," Salem recalled, "and do you know why Herod the Great's death came as such a blow?" Blank stares greeted his inquiry.

"Well," Salem shifted, "because all semblance of our national existence expired for the time being with him. You see, the old king's last will divided his kingdom among three of his sons he had not yet murdered: Herod Antipas, Herod Philip, and Archelaus. Herod Antipas governed Galilee and Perea. Herod Philip governed Ituraea and Trachonitis. Archelaus, who was almost as blood-minded as his father, governed Samaria, Idumea and Judea. His authority over these lands was confirmed to him by a decree of Caesar Augustus with the title of ethnarch, which is a little less than monarch. However, Archelaus' ineptitude offended Rome and he was replaced by Pilate."

Salem munched an oat cake while the boys swatted at flies. A skinny, bright-eyed boy asked, "How did Herod get Nazareth?"

"Nazareth is in Galilee, as you know, and thus became part of the dominions of Herod Antipas."

"And Herod Philip" asked a squinty-eyed nine year-old with a head of unruly brown curls, "what did he get?"

"Herod Philip got the rest of the Jewish lands east of the Jordan River. Both Herod Antipas and Herod Philip were given the title of tetrarch. Titles may not be that important," Salem waved his hand, "but another division of Herod the Great's will was. He willed that the authority of the Great Sanhedrin be diluted."

"The Great Sanhedrin? What is that?"

"The Great Sanhedrin is the supreme council and court of the Jews that decides the meaning of Mosaic Law. It is based in Yerushalayim and is dominated by the Sadducees."

"Sadducees?"

Och. These ragamuffins have so much to learn! But Salem was a willing teacher, the boys eager pupils. No one was in a hurry.

"The Sadducees are the party of the priests. They are the ecclesiastical judges and proffer a conciliatory attitude toward Rome. They deny that the oral law is authoritative and binding, attribute everything to free will, do not believe in angels or demons and reject the idea of a spiritual world. Sadducees accept only the five books of Torah and reject the concept of an afterlife because Moishe makes no mention of it."

The boys nodded roundly.

"Why did Herod Antipas want to lessen the Sanhedrin's power?" asked Abiud, a lanky, long-limbed lad of twelve.

"A good question, my boy," old Salem cackled, patting Abiud's head. "You see why history is so important? You boys must remember that Herod Antipas wanted to reduce the Great Council's influence and power because the Sanhedrin had opposed him. When he became king he executed forty-five of the Great Council's seventy-one members and reduced it to a purely religious council. That is why the council's authority is now limited to the territories of Archelaus: Judea, Samaria, and Idumea."

"The Great Sanhedrin has no authority anywhere else?"

"No where else," Salem nodded. "You and I and all inhabitants of Galilee and Perea are ruled by Herod Antipas and are thus not subject to the Great Sanhedrin."

"And Yeshua, can they get him here in Galilee?"

"No," Salem shook his head. "And Yeshua knows this. He and his followers are safe from the religious goon squads of the Sanhedrin so long as they remain within Galilee and Perea."

The boys exhaled a collective sigh of relief. Each youngster had met the young carpenter, whose bright eyes and strong arms were ever eager for a wrestling match, a game of tag or a swim in the stream Kasson. Outside Herod’s domain, however, vultures gathered and snakes coiled, waiting.

Seventeen

The midday sun beat down on the clay water pot balanced expertly atop two coiled braids of hair. The glass beads at her neck and the baubles upon her arms banged in the breeze, a gaudy euphony of discontent. She looked forward to the daily trip to Ya'cov's well as a cat anticipates a cold bath. Still, her partner needed water, and there were feet and hands to wash before the next meal.

Chava stood and peered about the countryside, taut and baking in the noonday heat. Olive groves and vineyards clothed the flanks of hilly Samaria. Rich forests of oak and terebinths grew to the west. Carobs, pistachios and oriental plane trees rose out of a dense undergrowth of myrtle, broom and other bushes such as acanthus, asphodel and wormwood. The young woman tipped her tired head slightly, *the Plain of Jezreel spreads her arms to the north, rich in wheat and warm-hued fields.*

Chava headed for Ya'cov's well. It was a half-mile tramp south of Sychar, on the high road from Yerushalyim where it curves to enter the valley between bold Mount Gerizim and squat Mount Ebal. *Ya'cov dug this well. It is deep, its water cool and refreshing.* And so it was. Both a cistern and a spring, the well was fed by surface water and by an underground source.

Wiping her brow and straightening her *keffiyah* against the prattling wind, the Samaritan woman trudged toward the well.

What is that? Her bright eyes could just make out a form on the ground, barely visible at the side of the well. *Is that a person?* The form shifted, sighing softly. *Is that a man? What is he doing sitting by the well, and at this time of day?*

True, Chava would have joined the other women at the well to draw water in the cool of the morning, but her last attempt was met by a torrent of sticks and pebbles.

"Away with you, tramp!" squawked one well-endowed matron, cupping a pebble into her hand.

"You'll not draw water from *this* well!" cried another, her hands already gripping a leather donkey switch. Two dozen townswomen, respectable matrons, shapely teenagers and young girls advanced, threatening.

But I just want to...

"Get away!" the baker's wife bellowed, "We know who you are and what you are. You're not fit to draw water with decent people!"

Please, I only need a little... just a few drops for washing.

Blessed art Thou, O Lord God, King of the Universe, who hast sanctified us with His commandments and has commanded us concerning the washing of hands.

Stones pelted her, dust stung her eyes. The women who were not throwing stones or refuse formed a protective ring around the well, a not-so-subtle girdle of public indignation designed to thwart any contamination that might arise from sharing the same air with Chava. She was, after all, a soiled woman. Everyone knew it. The impenetrable hedge of righteous ire was one she dared not attempt to breach.

A reject even among a rejected race, Chava cringed bitterly. *If I was lady of affluence, I would not have to draw my own water. Oh, for the means to order a servant to do this dreadful, lonely work!* She puled, painfully aware of her worn sandals, tattered dress and worn, chipped pot. Chava retreated behind a wall and waited for the women to finish drawing water before she attempted another approach.

Will the Lord reject us forever? Will he never show his favor again? Has his unfailing love vanished forever? Has his promise failed for all time?

Plumbing her mind for answers, the rejected woman waited until the others moved off, dozing under the noonday sun as children chased a kid goat across the street and swallows warbled in the dark mulberry trees.

Eighteen

Racing toward the water, Yo-hannah recalled a conversation with Levi, the tax-collector turned follower of Yeshua.

"Where can you find Yeshua?" Levi replied to her breathless inquiry. His face broke into a grin—crooked, but convivial—and Levi jabbed his finger at a cloud of dust and vivacious shouts. "Find the nearest game of tag, mancala, or spinning tops." Levi advised. "Find the children and you'll most likely find the master."

Yo-hannah's lungs begged for air, her breath tore out in sobs. *There! By the boys with the ball. Kicking, chasing, swinging with a stick.*

He waggled the stick and swung from his heels—and missed as cleanly as a blind man after a sparrow. The boys hooted him roundly. Head thrown back in peals of self-deprecating mirth, Yeshua bent over double, holding his sides as gales of laughter swept over him. Gasping for breath, he clapped a curly-headed youngster on the back and handed the stick to his team mate. It was Yeshua's turn to throw.

Yo-hannah spied the group near the shore. The man in the middle, tan, robust, with sturdy arms, sure hands and strong eyes. She had never seen this Yeshua before, but Yo-hannah hoped the tax-gatherer was right. If she could just get to him in time.

'Elohim! *Lord strong and mighty! Please*. *'Elyon*. God Most High. *El Olam*. *My son needs me...! God the Everlasting... Yahweh tsebhaoth, God of angelic hosts, King of Glory who rules*

heaven and earth in the interest of His people. 'Elroi. God who sees me.

Fading fast, sinking to the ground, Yo-hannah called on the Name she most needed.

But you, O Lord, are a compassionate
and gracious God,
... slow to anger,
... abounding in love
... and faithfulness.
Turn to me and have chesed on me.

Nearby, the Great Chesed heard the cry roll through the countryside like thunder. Mid-sentence with Judah and Levi and a group of children, Yeshua turned in response to a desperate petition unheard by any other. A matriarchal note of panic hung in the air, suspended and frozen. Yeshua's eyes swept the seashore, taking in the disciples, a young woman staggering toward the shore at a ragged run, an old man tottering after her at a distance, and Yames leaning over the limp body of a young boy.

Yeshua's lips moved wordlessly. Rephaiah coughed up water, gagged, and then gulped in air just as Yo-hannah collapsed, a hundred feet away.

Moments later Yo-hannah found herself upright, steady. Calm. No blind spots. No stars. No screaming pain inside her skull. In a haze of consciousness she saw a man. Tan, robust, strong eyes. Sturdy arms. Sure hands helped her to her feet. Then he was gone, leaving her as whole as a full moon.

It was gone. The headache packed up and left. But who did it? Who ordered the head *khamsin* to depart?

Who has taken away my affliction? Where is my healer, the One who heard my cry? Where is my Eldad, the One who turned to me?

Yo-hannah dashed to her son, sobbing, and gathered Rephaiah in grateful arms as a ragged band of onlookers mumbled something about "miraculous." A sweating Salem reached them and smiled heavenward.

It was a day or two before she confirmed his identity. Yohannah recalled the distant flap of Galilean homespun and the lavish fragrance of *chesed,* a bottomless well of lovingkindness poured out not once, but twice in one day by the One whose ears are never deaf to those who call upon Him.

Nineteen

Herod had a perennial problem with insecurity. He was hated by the Jews as a half-breed. One resolution to that problem was through bribery.

To ingratiate himself with the Jews, Herod decided to rebuild the temple. He cleared the entire site of Solomon's Temple and royal palaces, extending the work south so as to provide a platform four hundred yards long and three hundred yards wide. On this he built a temple twice as high as Solomon's. The courtyard was surrounded by magnificent colonnades. The whole place was one of the building wonders of ancient times.

In Yerushalayim Herod also built the Fortress Antonia. It stood at the northwest corner of the new temple and overlooked it. A further fortified palace was built on the western wall on the edge of the western hill. It was built around three towers. It was here that Herod would receive a prisoner he would never forget.

~

The most fertile area of Palestine, Galilee sprouts figs, dates, olive orchards, and shaggy walnut trees. Vineyards and wheat fields patchwork its rich hills, as do flax, from which linen is made. Sepphoris, the capital of Galilee, is the linen center of Palestine. The region itself also has a well-earned reputation for plentiful resistance to foreign rule. Herod learned this flinty truth first-hand.

As fiercely independent as an untrained donkey, the Galileans opposed Herod from the start. He, in turn, was as ruthless as he was merciless in establishing his authority, which he wrote in blood. And then Herod was called before the council at Yerushalayim, the Sanhedrin.

"Be sure to take a bodyguard with you," his father advised. Herod did.

Dominated by his enemies, the Sanhedrin charged Herod with illegally executing his opponents. While the council felt powerless to formally condemn Herod, the young ruler believed his life was in danger. He and his bodyguard fled the country for Syria.

"I swear by all the gods that they shall rue this day!" Herod swore, white-lipped and shaking with anger. Livid, he never forgot his humiliation.

Meanwhile, Julius Caesar's support of Herod dried up like a withered fig tree in the summer sun when the Roman world was again thrown into turmoil by Caesar's murder. Civil war broke out again. Brutus, Cassius and the other assassins took control of the east. Antipater was forced to do another about-face. Intent on demonstrating his value as a loyal ally, Antipater did everything possible to toady up to his new master. But the Jews had barely settled into the new regime when there was yet another change of course.

The instability of the Roman Empire encouraged Hyrcanus' rivals to make another bid for power. Herod's father was murdered. His nephew, Antigonus, invaded the country with Parthian support. Herod was recalled to help deal with the situation. He successfully repelled the invaders and was given a rapturous welcome by Hyrcanus, who betrothed him to his beautiful granddaughter, Miriam. Herod was already married, but this new marriage would give him the respectability he needed. He divorced his wife, Doris, and expelled her and Antipater, their son, from Yerushalayim.

Just when Herod's star seemed to be rising, however, news came of the defeat of Brutus and Cassius by Mark Antony and Caesar's nephew, Octavian. Antony now became ruler of the east. Hyrcanus was forced to do yet another about face. Accompanied by Phasael and Herod, he went helmet in hand with bags of money to make peace with his new master. Antony desperately needed all the support he could muster as he was expecting another attack by the Parthians. Hyrcanus was once again confirmed in his position. Phasael and Herod were both given the title "tetrarch."

The Parthians invaded Syria the next spring. Hyrcanus and Phasael were captured. Herod, foreseeing the worst, escaped from Jerusalem before the Parthians could scoop him into their net.

Herod arrived in Egypt in the autumn. He then followed Antony to Asia Minor and to Italy. In Rome, Herod appealed to Antony for help against Antigonus, backing up his plea with a large sum of money. Although the money helped, Antony recognized in Herod the only person who could possibly govern Judea and prove a reliable ally against the Parthians. He managed to convince Octavian, Caesar's adopted son, and the senate. Herod was nominated King of Judea.

Flanked by Antony and Octavian, Herod mounted the capitol where he offered sacrifice to Jupiter. This, Herod's first act as king, was to characterize his reign. For although he observed Jewish law in Judea, he was only half Jewish and a Gentile at heart.

Wasting no time, Herod sailed back to the east and landed at Acre in southern Syria. He was concerned for his relatives at Masada which had been under siege ever since he fled the city. Reduced to dire straits through lack of water, they had been saved by a downpour which had filled the cisterns. Herod collected a considerable force and with the support of the Romans, advanced on Galilee. Having secured the area, Herod pushed down the coast to Joppa. Once he had control of the port he marched into Idumea and relieved Masada.

Herod now turned to Yerushalayim, planning to lay siege to the city. It was mid-winter and the Roman commander insisted on withdrawing his troops to winter quarters due to a lack of supplies. Herod attempted to bring up provisions from Samaria, however, the Romans refused to close in.

Denied a quick victory in Yerushalayim, Herod decided to subdue the countryside. He marched north and stormed Galilee, then turned south into Samaria. He quelled revolts ruthlessly, slaughtering rebels, destroying their strongholds and plundering the countryside. Meanwhile, his Roman allies who had gone to help the governor of Syria defeated the Parthians in June.

Herod married Miriam the following spring before laying siege to Yerushalayim. He hoped that his marrying into the Hasmonean family would make him more acceptable to the people of Yerushalayim, who hated him for his half-Jewish, half-Gentile blood.

It did not.

So Herod immediately set about securing his throne. Ten years earlier he'd been charged with a capital offense by the Sanhedrin. Drinking deep the green draught of revenge, Herod executed forty-five of the Sanhedrin's seventy-five members and confiscated their property. This made a welcome addition to his treasury, and the council's power was thereafter restricted to religious matters.

Religion, Herod snorted, *is the purvey of dreamers, old women and little children. There's always some fool trying to stir up the people against Rome. Trying to bolster his claims as a 'deliverer' with tricks of healing and 'miracles' while working to remove me from my throne. Well,* he crossed his arms and fingered his sword, *we shall see about that.*

Twenty

Hadessa heard the stories trickling in from Galilee, Caesarea Philippi, Cana, and Bethany. Stories from the camel driver, a wine merchant, a laundress. Tales about a rabbi, perhaps a prophet, who healed a Canaanite woman's daughter, restored a widow's son to life, fed thousands from one boy's meager lunch. The rabbi had reportedly cleansed lepers, delivered demoniacs and even raised a man from the dead in Bethany.

"What sets him apart from any of the other demagogues, zealots and charlatans who declare themselves *Mashiah*?" Hadessa demanded. "Some of those pretenders attract large followings and cause plenty of Jewish blood to flow in the process." She shuddered at the recollections:

When Felix was governor of Judea, he had to deal with an Egyptian Jew who claimed he would bring down the walls of Yerushalayim with his own breath. This charlatan presented himself at the Mount of Olives east of the city, where Mashiah is supposed to appear. This Egyptian assembled four thousand fools to attack the city. Felix dispatched troops to take him prisoner. The lunatic was executed and his movement melted into the desert, disappearing faster than a moist mirage.

Hadessa numbered the "Jewish deliverer" stories on both hands and then some.

"So, how is this charismatic carpenter any different from the rest of these crazy religious zealots?" Hadessa asked the driver.

"He may have set down his tools and assumed his new identity, that of a wonder-working prophet. But he's not the first to do so, nor will this Yeshua be the last, I wager."

Would Yahweh ignore Judea, the heartland of His work for centuries, and choose instead the wretched region of Galilee for his mightiest of all works?

The driver seemed to hear Hadessa's gray thoughts as he shrugged, "Can anything good come out of Nazareth?"

~

But Hadessa remembered the stories and wondered. Rephaiah had narrowly escaped drowning at the seashore—"a miracle for him to be under the water so long and still be able to draw breath," some said. Yo-hannah's headaches had stopped for a time, but they returned as she worried ever more after her son. The young mother turned frantic every time Rephaiah left her side or wandered off for the briefest instant. Hadessa also knew that in gratitude for her healing and the safe return of her little one, Yo-hannah supported Yeshua and his followers out of her own purse.

"This Yeshua has done so much for me, how can I not show my gratefulness by sharing the bounty of my house?"

~

"What is he talking about?" Yames hissed a week later. Confusion wrapped his face like a bandage.

"I don't know, but I don't like the sound of it" Yo-hannan murmured, munching on a honey cake.

Yeshua's followers muttered amongst themselves, restless and bewildered. Judah dipped his hand into the money pouch, fingering another hundred taels of silver, newly arrived by courier, a gift from Chuza's wife. He deftly deposited the gift in support of Yeshua and his cortege into the leather money pouch that never left his side.

"What does Yeshua mean?" Yames questioned Judah. "He says we are all going up to Yerushalayim, and the Son of Man will be betrayed to the chief priests and the teachers of the law...?"

Judah arched a bushy black eyebrow. "... And they will condemn him to death and will turn him over to the Gentiles to be mocked and flogged and crucified."

A journey to Yerushalayim. Betrayal. Condemnation. Mockery, torture, an ignoble death? What did Yeshua mean? This story and more trickled in to a certain seaside villa where Passover preparations were underway.

"The young rabbi from Nazareth," Hadessa urged Chuza, "they say he fed thousands from one boy's lunch, that he makes the deaf to hear and the blind to see, the lame to walk. It seems that even the wind and the sea obey him." The ancient continued briskly, sensing Chuza's skepticism. "Well, what can it hurt if I take my lamb to see this rabbi? I've heard that Yeshua is heading toward the Holy City for Passover, as are we. I will take Yo-hannah, go ahead and secure lodging, make all the preparations. When you bring the boy later, all will be ready upon your arrival. Besides, my lamb isn't well."

Chuza nodded and looked away, eyes filling. Hadessa's voice softened. "Yo-hannah needs a change of scenery, something to take her mind off her troubles, eh?" Chuza met her gaze evenly, brightening a bit. "Besides, you've heard the stories about the rabbi from Nazareth. Maybe we can find him in Yerushalayim. Maybe... maybe." her voice trailed off.

"Maybe he can help her?" Chuza finished.

"Yes. If we can find him. Shall my lamb and I be off tomorrow?" Hadessa cocked one raisined eyebrow upward in what Chuza knew was more an imperative than an interrogative. The old woman decided. Not even the Steward of Herod the Tetrarch dared disagree.

Twenty-one

Out of the depths I cry to you, O Lord;
O Lord, hear my voice.
Let your ears be attentive to my cry for mercy.

The Mercy Seat. The *kapporeth* of the Ark. The covering of atonement. Not a mere lid, but the act and place of atonement and the accomplished atonement.

If you, O Lord, kept a record of sins, O Lord, who could stand? But with you there is forgiveness; therefore you are feared.

Veronica blanched at the thought. *Mercy* seat? Seat of *chesed*?

Twin cherubim wrought of gold faced each other, one at each side of the mercy seat. They overshadowed it with their wings, bending downward so that a wing of each extended over the mercy seat and met that of the other cherub. These angelic guardians symbolized the presence and unapproachability of Yahweh, whose glory was manifested between them. Yahweh thus dwelt in the midst of his people, and was present in the tabernacle to receive worship.

~

Veronica dipped her handkerchief into the wash basin, peered into the water and paled. Was it just a few years ago that she bloomed like a rose of Shar'on? Veronica's soft voice and soft eyes matched her soft heart. But twelve years of disease had withered the rose. Now she languished like a flower plucked from its stem.

Her formerly supple, nubile figure was bent and gaunt. Scarecrow-like, her gowns sagged on her spare, emaciated frame. Not even rich silks and fine Egyptian linen hid the ravages of her affliction. Her once-raven tresses streaked prematurely gray, Veronica's watery likeness reflected a raw-boned, gnarled grandmother instead of the glowing pulchritude of a thirty-four year old woman in the flush of femininity.

Veronica mused with King David, *I am in deep distress. Let me fall into the hands of the Lord, for his mercy is great; but do not let me fall into the hands of men.*

Twelve years of infirmity. Twelve years of ceremonial uncleanness. A fortune spent on useless doctors and dubious quacks whose skill or instruments or both could neither diagnose nor treat her condition, a chronic form of hemorrhage. More than a year's wages squandered on potions, lotions, herbs, vials. As was customary, she consulted the temple priests for a diagnosis, to no avail. If a prophet was to be had in all of Palestine, she would search him out, too. But where?

Twenty-two

I wait for the Lord, my soul waits,
and in His word I put my hope.

The Day of Atonement was an annual festival instituted by Moishe and held on the tenth day of the seventh month of the year. This day, *Yom Kippur*, was a day of national repentance and mourning. On this day, and on this day only, the high priest confessed the sins of the community and entered into the Most Holy Place of the tabernacle with the blood of the offering to make atonement for the people according to what the Lord had instructed Moishe:

The Lord said to Moishe: "Tell your brother Aaron not to come whenever he chooses into the Most Holy Place behind the curtain in front of the atonement cover on the ark, or else he will die, because I appear in the cloud over the atonement cover."

Veronica remembered.

The order of the ritual for the Day of Atonement was unswerving and unalterable. First the high priest entered the basin of the courtyard, removed his regular garments, washed himself and went into the Holy Place to put on the sacred linen garments. Then the high priest slaughtered a bull at the altar of burnt offering as a sin offering for himself and the other priests. He then went into the Most Holy Place with some of the bull's blood with incense and with coals from the altar of burnt offering. The incense was placed on the burning coals, and the smoke of the incense hid the ark from view.

The high priest then sprinkled the blood of an unblemished bullock on and before the atonement cover of the ark. He went outside the tabernacle and cast lots for two goats to see which was to be sacrificed and which was to be the scapegoat. At the altar of burnt offering the high priest killed the goat for the sin offering for the people, and for a second time he went into the Most Holy Place, this time to sprinkle the goat's blood in front of and on the atonement cover. He returned to the Holy Place and sprinkled the goat's blood there. He went outside to the altar of burnt offering and sprinkled it with the blood of the bull (for himself) and of the goat (for the people). While in the courtyard, he laid both hands on the second goat. This symbolized the transfer of Yisrael's sin and the removal of the nation's guilt. The high priest then sent the goat out into the desert. After accomplishing this task, the man who took the goat away washed himself and his clothes outside the camp before rejoining the people.

Then the high priest entered the Holy Place to remove his sacred garments. He went out to the basin to wash and put on his regular priestly clothes. As a final sacrifice, he went out to the great altar and offered a ram as a burnt offering for himself, and another ram for the people. The conclusion of the entire day was the removal of the sacrifices for the sin offerings to a place outside the camp, where they were burned, and there the man who performed this ritual bathed and washed his clothes before rejoining the people.

Thus the high priest made atonement for his sins and those of the nation in the presence of the covenant law, the covenant carried down from Mount Sinai by Moishe, which was written on tables of stone and laid in the Ark.

The ritual was rich with imagery and symbolism. Inside this most sacred of all sacred places, the burning of incense, symbol of accepted worship, was conducted in the presence of Yahweh. The pungent fragrance rose and enveloped the mercy seat in a cloud. The blood from the sacrifice sprinkled on a variety of objects and people atoned for sin and uncleanness. The blood sacrifice "covered" the sin, thereby hiding it from the sight of a holy God. Even the words in the ritual meant something significant.

Scapegoat. Sin symbolically transferred to a live animal which then carried it into the desert, typifying the permanent removal of sin.

Sacrifice. The act of sacrifice expressed faith, adoration, and repentance—a sincere acknowledgement of guilt before God, and a resolute turning away from sin in which the sinner identifies himself with the gracious act of God in redeeming him.

Kippur. From the Hebrew root, K-P-R, meaning "covering." The Greek *katallage* means reconciliation. When sin is covered, reconciliation is effected.

Covering. Sacrifice. Satisfaction. Reconciliation. *Where*? *When? Who?*

Has God forgotten to be merciful? Has He in anger withheld his compassion?

Veronica stared at the aging, infirm reflection in the water basin. A terrible sadness poured over her, hollow and soul-suffocating. *Incomprensible One, where is Your mercy now?*

Twenty-three

"He's a non-Jew, an Idumean. They're an Arab people," Chuza whispered to his wife.

The day had been full: caravans of camels returning with linens from Egypt, servants requiring training, bills of sale to be finalized, totals to be tallied, accounts to be rendered and bottom lines to be balanced. Chuza was tired, but Yo-hannah insisted on knowing more about his master. Knowing her tenderness for children which far transcended his own understanding, the Steward of Herod Antipas wondered how much he should tell his wife. Yo-hannah was already delicate, physically and mentally.

Is she strong enough for the full story? Chuza decided to sidestep that question for the moment and begin with something a little more mundane, like progeny.

"According to the Jewish scriptures, Idumeans are the progeny of Esau, the twin brother of Jacob who cheated his brother out of his blessing. That's why Idumeans are called `Edomites' by the Jews, who also call Herod the 'Edomite Servant' because of his servile relationship to Rome. Are you following all this, my dear?"

Yo-hannah nodded, and then replied thoughtfully, "Yet among Greeks and Romans Herod became known as 'Herod the Great'?"

"Yes, a title he earned for overcoming his enemies and extending the borders of his kingdom over all the land of Palestine."

"It didn't seem to win him any favors here."

"No, nor did any of Herod's attempts to mollify his Jewish subjects."

"You mean the temple?"

Chuza laced his fingers behind his neck and leaned back on a silk *pulvinus* next to his wife.

"Ah yes, the temple. The most monumental of all of Herod's projects, reconstructing that great temple in Yerushalayim. A truly magnificent edifice. A common saying amongst Jews is that anyone who has not seen the temple in Yerushalayim has not seen anything really beautiful."

"A true statement," Yo-hannah observed, recalling descriptions of the innermost court of the temple complex at Yerushalayim, a court open only to Jewish men.

The sacred ambience of the place was overwhelming: light flickering from the candlesticks, rainbow hues of cherubim embroidered in scarlet, purple, blue, and gold. The golden altar of incense glistening in the light. The priest poured the incense on white-hot coals and the sacrifices rose to Yahweh, swathed in the sweet fragrance of believing prayer. The aroma of worship swirled from and into every corner.

"Even building that splendid temple did not diminish Jewish hostility for Herod," her husband brought Yo-hannah back to the silk cushions, "because they detested the taxes he levied to pay for it!"

"Meanwhile, Herod was killing his children, wives, and other relatives and friends until the day he died. Out of his ever-increasing suspicions of essentially everyone, Herod ultimately forbade his subjects to meet, walk or eat together in groups of three or more. He stationed spies in cities, towns and villages to see if anybody met contrary to his edicts. Those accused of doing so were dragged away and never seen again."

Yo-hannah recalled the Fortress Antonia in Yerushalayim and the great numbers of prisoners the rocky tower seemed to devour. She knew that in his early years as king, Herod erected an imposing fortress in Yerushalayim where its towers overlook the sacred precincts of the temple. Herod called the stronghold the Fortress

Antonia, in honor of his friend and patron Mark Antony.

Crouched behind a high stone wall, the fortress was large and imposing. A massive door guarded the entrance, where soldiers stood at attention like blind, mute statues. The hall beyond was white marble, lit by silver lamps on slim standards suspended from a forest of columns. Because the Fortress Antonia dominated the city and thus represented the power of Rome, its every stone was a weight upon the hearts of Yerushalayim's people.

"You must understand, my dear, that my master's father was in the grip of a fatal cancer. Life was ebbing out of Herod the Great, seeping away as water through a sieve. Then word came to him that a son born of the line of David would succeed his throne!"

Yo-hannah blinked, failing to grasp the connection. The midday sun dripped off the trees like melting butter. Yo-hannah's chin trembled even as she arched her eyebrows into a searching expression and bid her husband continue.

"Naturally, King Herod was convinced that the dynasty he had founded was to be thrust aside! Can you imagine? His Highness, the finger of Rome, thrust aside by some mystic Jewish rubbish about a coming king?" Chuza paused dryly. He downed half his cup of wine before adding, "Herod the Great was a loyal ally of Rome and a pragmatic ruler of his people. To preserve his throne, Herod ordered the slaughter of the innocents in Bethlehem, the birthplace and ancestral home of David."

The wife of Chuza pondered aloud, "That dusty little town in the hill country of Judah, which Romans call Judea, birthplace of a king?" Chuza shrugged and poured himself more wine.

"Improbable as it seems, the prophet Micaiah foretold this birth: *But you, Bethlehem Ephrathah, though you are small among the clans of Judah, out of you will come for me one who will be ruler over Yisrael, whose origins are from old, from ancient times.*

Micaiah? Yo-hannah searched her memory. That unsophisticated rustic? *The peasant prophet who always had before him the bent backs and wizened lives of the poor and the downtrodden? Micaiah, prophesying about Bethlehem? Ephratath? Fruitful, house of bread?* Yo-hannah hid her cynicism behind an inquiry,

"How in the world did this 'king' get to be born in that backwater village?"

"Well my dear, no doubt you remember several years ago—or perhaps you were too young then, but Hadessa could tell you--Caesar Augustus issued a decree that a census should be taken of the entire Roman world. Caesar had his purposes in issuing this edict. He wanted to tax everyone."

"Not much has changed," Yo-hannah sighed.

"… and the census would also be used as the basis for issuing calls for military service. Since Jews are exempt from serving in the Roman legions, Caesar's sole interest in them was for what wealth he could extract from them."

Chuza paused thoughtfully while Yo-hannah sipped a steaming brew of tea flavored with lemon and honey. He settled back further into the silk cushions of the lilac scented chamber, head tilted back thoughtfully.

"Quirinius was governor of Syria back then," Chuza continued, "and the reason I recall that is because Judea was beneath Syria in the Roman order."

So God Most High had Caesar run an errand for Him? Mighty Caesar—a piece of lint on the parchment of prophecy?

"In obedience to Caesar's command," Chuza continued, "the man Yosef, espoused to a certain Miryam from Galilee, a poor peasant girl, returned with his expectant wife to the city of his ancestor, King David."

"And then what...?"

Twenty-four

Have mercy on me, O God, have mercy on me,
for in you my soul takes refuge.

Veronica had loved their trips to the great temple complex in the Holy City. The area covered by the temple complex was a leveled platform of one thousand feet square. The main entrance was on the east, through Solomon's gate. Into this magnificent porch or outer courtyard any Jew or Gentile could enter, hence the name, the Court of the Gentiles.

The money changers and traders assembled here. Business was good. Jews and proselytes had to pay an annual, half-shekel temple tax. Shortly before a festival, money changers set up stalls all over the land to collect the tax—and line their own pockets in the process.

North of the Gentile enclave was a raised enclosure surrounded by a four foot high marble screen. Latin and Greek inscriptions forbade Gentiles to pass beyond this screen under pain of death.

Another superb porch, the Beautiful Gate, led into this courtyard. Veronica used to walk into this inner preserve, also called the Court of the Women because Jewish women gathered there for any rituals which affected them. She was not allowed to go any further but could look into the inner courtyards from a raised platform.

Still more steps led through the Nicanor Gate and the Court of Yisrael. Only Jewish men entered here. Cleansed lepers and women coming for purification after childbirth presented themselves before a priest at the Nicanor Gate but did not pass through.

Beyond the Court of Yisrael was the Court of the Priests. Set into the surrounding walls were storage and work chambers for everything to do with temple service, including a place for animals due for sacrifice. There were rooms for the comfort of the priests, cooking, dining, and sleeping quarters. There was also the hall where the Sanhedrin sat and other halls for official occasions.

In the Priests' Court stood the altar of burnt offering and the huge brass laver. Water was drawn up from one of the many cisterns supplying the temple. The cisterns were supplied with water carried by aqueduct from pools which pockmarked the land some miles outside Yerushalayim.

~

"How much water can one temple require?" Veronica once asked Yitzhak.

"Remember, wife," he explained, "water is needed for ritual washings and other cleanings. The temple authorities have no wish to be stingy about hygiene in this hot climate." Yitzhak went on to note the constant swilling of blood and refuse that ran down in the Kidron Valley through a complex drainage system, resulting in one of the most fertile spots in the country.

~

The temple service opened with the prayer leader reciting the three paragraphs of the *Shema*, the great credal declaration of the unity of God: *Hear, O Yisrael, the Lord is our God, the Lord is One*. The *Shema* was introduced by the *Ahavah Rabbah*:

With great love you have loved us, O Lord our God, and great and overflowing tenderness have you shown us.

Then the leader led worshippers in the eighteen benedictions of the *Amidah.* Of great antiquity, the *Amida*h is the most important and best loved prayer in Judaism. Veronica's favorite blessing was the second:

Thou sustainest the living with lovingkindness, revivest the dead with great mercy, supportest the falling, healest the sick, freest the bound, and keepest thy faith to them that sleep in the dust. Who is like unto thee, Lord of mighty acts?

~

Revival? Support? Healing, freeing, faithing, mighty acts? The sweet and tender mercy of racham? Veronica dragged herself from past to present. *When? Where? From whom?*

Desperate for all, Veronica once considered pagan charms or the incantations offered by Simon, the local sorcerer. Staring at the basin, her eyelids quivered. *I have waited years for Yahweh's mercy to show itself. Where is it? Where is Your great love now? Where are YOU?*

Torah finally won out. Veronica's ancestors won out: *"You shall have no others gods before me. You shall not make for yourself an idol in the form of anything in heaven above or on the earth beneath or in the waters below. You shall not bow down to them or worship them; for I, the Lord your God, am a jealous God..."*

No. Veronica would not, could not go to the sorcerer. Even if the Most High had no mercy for her, she could not forsake her heritage.

I am doomed to suffer this wretched, wasting disease until I die. Her lips trembled. *Then let death come soon, Elohim. I can bear neither the shame nor the pain any longer. End it. End me. Please.*

Twenty-five

He does not treat us as our sins deserve
or repay us according to our iniquities.
For as high as the heavens are above the earth,
so great is his love for those who fear him.

Swallows chirped. Insects whined. Diana and Phoebe laughed from the reedy river bank where they sat swapping gossip. Beautiful, shapely, and simple, Diana waved playfully at Gaius. Her husband smiled blandly, returning her wave. *A wife is a luscious diversion and a pleasant past time*, Gaius thought, *but a soldier's duty is to his commander; my full allegiance belongs to Rome, and Rome alone.*

His thoughts turned toward an incident he overheard at a roadside tavern. Between bites of stale barbels and greasy pottage, pearls of dialogue and detail were strung by a fellow traveler.

"What are you thinking?" Julius prodded, noting Gauis' distraction.

"Just... thinking."

"Good. Thinking is a virtue. But what about?"

For some reason he couldn't explain, Gauis hesitated at recounting the story to Julius. It had to do with that Yeshua fellow again. Julius read his mind.

"The 'wonder-working prophet' from Nazareth?" he scoffed.

"What's he done now?"

Julius knew him too well. He'd never been able to conceal anything from him for long.

"Well," Gauis grunted, sitting. "It has to with that Yeshua, a wicked woman, and stones."

~

Dipped into a palette of cherry, peppermint and ginger, sunrise rinsed rosy fingers across Yerushalayim's hills that morning. Daybreak's iridescent seeds bloomed into a bouquet of mauve, umber and yellow as the sun stretched and yawned.

Teaching a cluster of men in the forecourt of the temple, Yeshua's morning lesson was interrupted by a shrill cry. Whether the screech came from the hornet's nest of Pharisees swarming toward the circle in short, angry strides or from the screaming, cursing woman they dragged with them, no one could tell.

Looking up at the disturbance, Yeshua stopped speaking mid-sentence. He stood as the woman was hurled into their midst. Bruised, her knees skinned and her shift torn, the disheveled woman crouched like a caged cat, spitting and cursing in the center of a wolfish circle.

A lanky, leathery Pharisee adjusted the *tephillin* prayer boxes on his forehead and left arm. Kenan was one of the *Haverim*. This sect of Pharisees was punctilious about ceremonial ablutions like washing hands and kitchen utensils. Kenan tithed on all he ate, bought or sold, including common garden herbs. He did not eat with ordinary folks lest something had not been tithed and some items Kenan would not buy from or sell to them.

Stabbing a bony finger at the Accused, the *Haverim* snarled, "We found this woman in the act of committing adultery."

Another Pharisee, portly, pristine, and red-faced, huffed, "The law of Moishe commands that any woman taken in adultery must be stoned." Lathered, Nobai added in his detergent voice, "What do you say?"

The sun ripened like a citrus bloom in spring. Fresh goat's

milk spattered into a bucket as a nearby child performed the morning milking. Willow leaves fluttered. Satin clouds crocheted a cobalt canopy overhead. But here, inside the ring of accusers, the only color was scarlet.

The *Hasidim* were also among the accusers. These "pious ones" stood for the uncompromised purity of Judaism. Repudiating all Gentile ways, they interpreted their religion so strictly that other people nicknamed them "Separatists'" or *Perushim,* from the Hebrew *parush*; hence *Pharisees.*

~

"I'd have liked to have heard this Yeshua's reply to those sulky Separatists myself," Gaius muttered, wondering if the stories were true. Rumor had it that the same carpenter who regularly sliced into the Jewish religious leaders also extended an unexpected tenderness toward women who had misstepped.

Julius sat up suddenly, spilling wine and green grapes. "Well, what *could* he say? If this Yeshua told them the woman should be stoned, they would have done it then and there, and he would've been guilty of inciting them to kill her-- murder under Roman law."

Gaius nodded. "But if he said she should not be stoned, then the Pharisees would tell everyone he had contradicted the word of their god, that he condones adultery."

"A perfect trap."

"So what did he do?"

"He stooped and wrote in the dust with one finger."

"He did *what*?" Julius' square jaw dropped, astonishment dousing his ruddy features.

"He wrote in the dust."

"Wrote what?" his wife, Phoebe, asked. So engrossed in their conversation, the centurions hadn't noticed the approach of their wives. Henna-rinsed, rouged Phoebe sat down, wide-eyed and equally confounded.

"I don't know. It seems that no one could read it except the Pharisees." Gaius suppressed the urge to burst out laughing as he imagined the scene.

"Then Yeshua stood," Gaius continued. "He said, `let him who is without sin cast the first stone.' Yeshua even held out a rock to them, daring them. He looked them right in the eyes, one Pharisee after another. That Nobai pulled his beard so hard, folks thought his face would fall off!"

"Then what?" Diana asked, voice as sweet and lilting as a dulcimer.

"The Pharisees left, one by one, the oldest filing out first. Nobai led the exodus."

"You're jesting!" Phoebe shook her head as a thin, contemptuous smile rippled features. "Those crafty old foxes? Just giving up and leaving?"

"Yes, they drifted away until only Yeshua and the woman were left, alone."

"Then what?" Julius queried, perched on the edge of the grass. This was almost as good as a circus spectacle.

"The others filed out, leaving just the two of them."

~

He, she. Stainless, soiled. Spotless, seductress. *Person grata, persona non.* Hers, a bedraggled life littered with broken commandments. His, a sinless soul observing two groups of people: those who knew they were sinners and those who didn't. Yeshua offered her a trade. Her condemnation for his compassion.

"Woman, where are they? Has no one condemned you?"

"No one, sir."

"Then neither do I condemn you." Yeshua held out his hand, open. No stone in sight. "Go now and leave your life of sin."

~

Creaking and rusty as an old gate, a memory stirred in Gaius' mind as Phoebe snorted. What had Arieh claimed about his "Unknown God"?

"Well," Phoebe hauled Gaius back from his musings with a wagging, jeweled finger, "if they didn't catch and punish the man for adultery, then they shouldn't try to kill the woman for it, either."

Julius sighed. "I'm afraid you miss the point, my dear. The conflict was about power. Should this carpenter prove to be their Mashiah, what place can these `pious ones' expect in his kingdom? And what kind of kingdom would it be under one who chastises them publicly and regards their traditions with such distaste? Besides," he paused gingerly, "whatever else he may be, this Nazarene is no dunderhead. He knows full well that the same *Haverim* and *Hasidim* who accused the woman will never forgive him for making them out to be fools and hypocrites."

Julius gave Gauis a quick nod. His brother centurion caught the intent and returned it.

Twenty-six

Concussed with fear, stalked by chagrin, Veronica's stomach somersaulted. Tears welled up in her eyes. She bit her lip, determined to fight the watery rebels back. Veronica gagged on the dust kicked up by so many sandals as despair overran her dikes of self-discipline and slid down her cheeks in wet canals.

Do you remember me, Adonai? Do you know my name?

~

Yet the Lord longs to be gracious to you;
he rises to show you compassion.

Yo-hannah shuddered, pulling the coverlet to her chin. Her blood roared in her ears. Her head throbbed. Perspiration glistened on the young mother's brow as an icy coldness took her. She pulled the coverlet to her chin. It was yet the dead of night.

In her half-asleep, half-awake haze, Chuza's wife heard it again. Moaning. The dull, piercing wail of deep loss. Stifled sobs. Stumbling from her bed, the auburn-haired woman padded barefoot to the window and halted. The night outside was as limpid as water, brisk but not yet cold. Scents of apple, lavender and cinnamon wafted to her nose on a ticklish midnight breeze. She peeked past the curtains, trembling. The wailing stopped.

"I must be going mad!" the slender, linen-clad lady muttered, dabbing perspiration from her face and throat. It was the fifth time in as many days that the eerie sound awakened her. Wrenching her from a sound slumber and thoughts of her darling son, the muffled sobs rose and fell with the moon. Yet each time she crept to the window to detect the source of the unnerving sound, it stopped. Vanished like morning fog in strong sunshine.

Instinctively, Yo-hannah hurried to Rephaiah's bed, her breath and heart slowing as she gazed upon his cherubic slumber. She ran a maternal hand over Rephaiah's soft cheek and hair, kissed the boy and tucked his coverlet tighter before returning to bed beside her husband for another restless night of disembodied sorrow. The *khamsin* inside her head began to blow.

Adonai, do you remember me?

Twenty-seven

The temple hill, sometimes known as "Mount Moriah," was formerly the threshing floor of Araunah the Jebusite. David purchased the floor and erected an altar on it. David's son, Solomon, built the Great Temple in Yerushalayim to honor the One God. Temple stones gleamed in the early morning and glowed gold in the afternoon. At night, fiery stars lit up each stone as it reflected moonlight.

Both city and temple were beautiful, and because they were beautiful, kings fought for the site and foreigners invaded it: Babylonians, Greeks, and Romans, Worshippers of false gods, idols and omens, the Romans brought stones and battering rams that sundered the old walls of the city. Romans swords made the streets run red. Those nights were a terror, but not nearly as terrible as The Night in Bethlehem.

~

Yo-hannah knew the story but she wanted to hear it again, from Chuza. He glanced around, lowered his head and confided in a conspiratorial whisper, "Gentiles from the east, from Persia, came to Yerushalayim and asked, 'Where is the one who has been born king of the Jews?' Not that he would become a king later on, but that he was *born* a king." Chuza peered at his wife to make sure she understood this significance. Yo-hannah nodded intently.

"King Herod heard this and was disturbed. When Herod was disturbed, so was all of Yerushalayim, and for good reason! His reign was soaked in blood."

Yo-hannah shuddered, remembering the wailing and mourning of her dreams.

"Herod called together all the chief priests and teachers of the law and asked where this king would be born. They told him as I told you, as the prophet said, 'In Bethlehem of Judah.' Then Herod called these Magi, wise men, and bade them search for the child 'so that I may come and worship him too.'"

"Did they find the child, the one born a king?"

How can this be? Would God bypass the majestic city of Yerushalayim for the lowly village of Bethlehem?

"Yes," Chuza replied, "they followed a star which stopped over a house. And there they saw the child with his mother Miryam, and they bowed down and worshipped him."

"But what happened to the baby?"

"He was well nigh two years old by the time the Magi found him. They were warned in a dream not to go back to Herod, and they returned to their country by another route."

Yo-hannah let out a sigh of relief, but she sensed the story was not yet finished. "And then...?"

"When Herod realized that the wise men had outwitted him, he was furious! He gave orders to kill all the boys in Bethlehem and the vicinity that were two years old and under, in accordance with the time he had learned from the Magi."

"And the baby?"

"His mother's husband was warned in a dream, told to flee to Egypt, which they did. The child escaped the sword. But the rest of Bethlehem's little ones did not."

"Bethlehem?" Yo-hannah queried in an incredulous contralto.

"Yes, Bethlehem," Chuza replied. "The City of David. The town south of Yerushalayim, resting on the slopes of those limestone hills which are honeycombed with caves. It's where the slaughter of the innocents took place."

Yo-hannah watched Rephaiah chase a ball. She had heard the rumors, the whispers. Yo-hannah simply refused to believe anything so wicked and ruthless could occur in the City of David—even by one as wicked and ruthless as Herod the Great, the father of her husband's employer. But it didn't surprise her. His son, the tetrarch of Galilee, had Yo-hannan the Baptizer arrested and beheaded.

She had heard of this Baptizer whose scathing diatribes stirred up unrest in Galilee and Perea like flies scattering from a horsetail swish. Yo-hannan's diurnal railings against evil in high places included Herod Antipas, whom he denounced for various improprieties. These included Herod's marriage to the silver-tongued, lizard-lidded Herodias, whose hooded eyes and pinched face resembled a coiled cobra's. The venomous queen was the tetrarch's niece and the former wife of his brother Herod Philip. The marriage was considered incestuous by the Jews.

The Baptizer, wild-eyed and bushy-bearded, traipsed out of the desert and declared that the Roman Empire and the rights of the Herodian lines of royalty would all be set aside in a new kingdom to be established by Yahweh. Well, talk about adding fuel to the fire! Sermons like that in Palestine strike like lightning on dry scrub. Making matters even more incendiary, Yo-hannan proclaimed himself the herald of the new king with declarations like, "I am the voice of one calling in the desert, 'Prepare the way for the Lord, make straight paths for him.'"

Chuza continued. "What really set Antipas off was when Yo-hannan, cousin of Yeshua, said of Yeshua, "Look, the Lamb of God, who takes away the sin of the world!" The Baptizer was making reference to a passage from the prophet Isaias, "... and the Lord has laid on him the iniquity of us all. ... he was led like a lamb to the slaughter..."

Did Yo-hannan's allusion to Yeshua being the Lamb of God foreshadow the course of the Nazarene's life? Yo-hannah mulled it over in her mind. *Our scriptures state that forgiveness of sin requires a blood sacrifice. Has Yeshua accepted the role of sacrificial lamb—as ascribed to him by Yo-hannan? Are the rumors true?*

She recalled Herod Antipas' treatment of the Baptizer. Fearing that Yo-hannan was beginning to evince revolutionary, if not messianic, incantations, Herod ordered him arrested and locked up in the fortress of Machaera. Herodias resorted to guile to get the Baptizer beheaded.

If the outspoken Yo-hannan met such a fate, what was to become of his candid cousin?

Twenty-eight

His features marked him as a Jew. She sighed heavily and paused, weighing whether or not to approach the well. If a lone *woman* rested at the well this time of day, Chava would have weighed her options more carefully. But this was a man, and she knew men. She would neither budge nor retreat. Besides, it was hot and she was thirsty. She sauntered to the far side of the well and balanced her clay water pot on the lip of the well.

"Will you give me a drink?"

The man's request was a strange one. *He is clearly a rabbi* Chava thought, noting his clothing. *But Jews do not make common use of vessels with Samaritans!* Chava remembered the Jewish gibes and reproaches she had endured as a child:

"He who eats the bread of a Samaritan is as he who eats swine's flesh."

"No Samaritan shall be made a proselyte."

"They have no share in the resurrection of the dead."

Who is this man, this Jewish rabbi seated at the curb of Ya'cov's well in the noontide heat? He not only speaks to me, but he makes a request. He is thirsty. Shall I give him a drink?

There was something about this man. Eyes the color of melted chocolate widened in astonishment. "You are a Jew and I am a Samaritan woman. How can you ask me for a drink?"

Chava shrugged her shoulders. *It's not my fault he neglected to bring water. Thirsty travelers should know better than to wander without a wineskin, or approach a well without a pot.* Chava turned to go, but his eyes caught her, arrested her. She knew she could not refuse and silently offered him water.

He took the bowl she gingerly extended, never taking his eyes off her. She was not used to that sort of look. His was a gentle look, kind and somewhat sad. His voice was as soft and as cool as well water. "If you knew the gift of God and who it is that asks you for a drink, you would have asked him and he would have given you living water." His voice rang like a bell and carried a slight inflection marking him as a native of Galilee.

This man is a rabbi. Why is he talking with me in public? Is this not in direct contradiction to the rabbinic precepts?

Chava knew that according to the precepts, a man should not speak in public to his own wife, and that the words of the Law should be burned rather than taught publicly to a woman.

If he is a rabbi or teacher sent from Yahweh, why would he talk to me, a woman? I am a Samaritan and a sinner.

She was. Somehow she knew he knew, too. Yet his voice and manner gripped her. Chava did not understand his message. *Was this truly an ordinary fellow? He speaks with authority.* "Are you greater than Ya'cov, our ancestor?" *Who are you?*

Having had five successive husbands—or "customers," as the rumors ran--she was not easily bested in conversation. Tossing her head and squinting into the hills, Chava wanted to know where the well better than Ya'cov's was, from which she could secure this "living water."

Thinking in terms of the well beneath her, Chava was puzzled. *He has no skin to pour water from, nor any utensil for drawing out, and the well is deep.* At the bottom was the living, running water fed by a spring. *Can this rabbi hope to conjure up what Ya'cov secured only by hard toil? He would be even greater than our ancestor if he can do this!*

"Sir, you have nothing to draw water with, and the well is deep. Where can you get this living water? Are you greater than our father Ya'cov, who gave us this well...?"

Please, I only need a little... just a few drops for washing.

He motioned to the well. "Everyone who drinks this water will be thirsty again, but whoever drinks the water I give him will never thirst."

Chava's mouth fell open. Bees buzzed. Dust traced its fine outline on her nose and hair. A desert wind moaned through the palms, rattled some dates.

"Indeed, the water I give him will become in him a spring of water welling up to eternal life."

No more trudges to this ghastly well! No more arduous drawing and hauling! LIVING water that never runs dry! Where is it?! What is his source? Where is his spring? Is his offer that of surface or underground water?

Her eyes blazed with eagerness. Thirst in the desert of Sychar was never permanently sated. Well water had to be drawn and drunk again and again. *Who are you? What is your name?*

"Sir, give me this water so that I won't get thirsty and have to keep coming here to draw water." She certainly wouldn't miss running the gossip gauntlet each day that her walk to the well entailed.

I only need a little...

"Go, call your husband and come back."

Twenty-nine

Bits jangled. Horses stamped and lunged. Shouts rang out on Bethlehem streets. Soldiers dismounted, unsheathing deadly weapons. Swords glinted in the moonlight. Fathers fought and failed. Maternal shrieks rent the night as Herod's soldiers ripped infants from protective arms. Blades slashed. Blood spurted. How many boys aged two years or less would never see the dawn?

The words of the prophet Jeremias were fulfilled: *A voice is heard in Ramah, mourning and great weeping, Rachel weeping for her children and refusing to be comforted, because her children are no more.*

So. The wailing in the wind. The sobs in the night. Mothers weeping for dead children slaughtered by a ruthless king whose god was ambition and whose knees bowed to Rome.

~

Chuza shifted uneasily, scrutinized a far-off olive branch and lowered his voice, "What you've heard is true, my dove. Herod, King of Judea, ordered the slaying of the infants of Bethlehem in an effort to save his own hide. Every male child aged two years and under was slain. You recall Herodium, visible from the southeast of Bethlehem? "

Yo-hannah nodded, envisioning the symmetrical mountain with flattened top which can be seen from either the hills of Yerushalayim or those of Bethlehem. A large, elaborate, circular palace-fortress straddles the mountain, serving dual duty as both the king's residence and a defensive position.

"Herodium serves as a constant and bitter reminder of King Herod, who, in his old age, slew all the little boys of Bethlehem." Chuza remembered when Herod died in Jericho. His elaborate funeral cortege included almost his entire army and wound its way to Herodium, where the ruthless king's body was interred upon a golden bier embroidered with precious stones. But Yo-hannah recalled something else, a wailing in the wind that left her heart dry and her head throbbing.

The young mother knew weeping for lost children all too well. She swept Rephaiah into her arms as if to shield him from impending danger. Perhaps because of her own losses, the babies who had died before they lived, Yo-hannah felt the story press in upon her like a live saber. How she knew the anguish of a grieving mother bereft of her children! Grief to make one go mad, to bottle up one's mind, beat upon one's brow and cause one's head to explode!

The razoresque pain of an impending migraine stabbed at her eye sockets even as Yo-hannah pressed her only living son's tousled curls so close to her bosom that Chuza had to loosen her grip lest the child suffocate. Rephaiah. *Yahweh has healed.* The boy slept peacefully as his mother watered his coverlet with her tears.

~

Yeshua departed Samaria after two days and journeyed into Galilee, where he healed the son of a court officer in Capernaum, Yeshua's home during much of his ministry. Then Yeshua returned to Nazareth, to the synagogue which he and his family had always attended. It was Shabbat. As a local member who had gained fame and notoriety, Yeshua was asked to lead the prayers and preach.

He stood on the *bimah*, surrounded by the worshippers and facing the Ark to recite the *Shema. Hear, O Yisrael: the Lord our God, the Lord is One*. Then he led the worshippers in the eighteen benedictions of the *Amidah.* Yeshua paused as if he heard something. A whisper. Then he recited the second blessing with closed eyes:

> *Thou sustainest the living with lovingkindness, revivest the dead with great mercy, supportest the falling, healest the sick, freest the bound, and keepest thy faith to them that sleep in the dust. Who is like unto Thee, Lord of mighty acts?*

He stood aside while the attendant handed the Torah scroll, already open at the right place, to the person chosen to read the Torah. Yeshua then returned and read from the book of the prophet Isaias:

> *The Spirit of the Lord is on me; because he has anointed me to preach good news to the poor. He has sent me to proclaim freedom for the prisoners and recovery of sight for the blind, to release the oppressed, to proclaim the year of the Lord's favor.*

He rolled up the scroll, returned it to the attendant and sat down. The eyes of all in the synagogue were fixed upon him. Yeshua began to speak. "Today this scripture has been fulfilled—in the things of which you have heard."

"Who is this?" Benyamin the scribe pressed his crisp white garments against his ornate chair, the best seat in the synagogue. "Is this Yosef's son?" the snowy-haired scribe sputtered indignantly as snide remarks about the local carpenter and his simple, working class background and dubious parentage flew around the room. "Who does he think he is, sauntering into our synagogue with these pretentious claims?"

"We've heard about how you healed the boy in Capernaum on the north shores of the Sea of Galilee. Why not heal someone here, too?"

"Yes, if you're really who you say you are, why not show us a miracle to prove your mashianic claims?"

Yeshua looked out at the people. There was Jared, always slow to pay for work done. Behind him sat Micah who had cheated his father out of an entire flock of sheep. The next row seated Ruben, Isaac and Isa, notorious womanizers and cheats. Up above were

Naomi, Mara and Recab, whose tedious tongues never stopped wagging. The loquacious trio peddled lies, rumor and gossip like *suk* merchants at the bazaar, dividing friends and families with half-truths and wheedling insinuations.

The synagogue of Nazareth burst at the seams with liars, drunkards, gluttons, slanderers and cheats. The unkind, the quarrelsome and covetous, the malicious and mean, the petty and puerile. He knew them all, yet Yeshua refused to bite the bait.

Would it make any difference? Yeshua eyed the crowd ruefully, then withdrew from the synagogue and started to walk away. Furious, Benyamin led the charge to throw Yeshua out of the city and off a hill until Yeshua passed through their midst and went down to Capernaum by the sea.

Thirty

You are my hiding place;
you will protect me from trouble
and surround me with songs of deliverance.

Chava knew what Torah said against adultery. She was now living with a man who was not her husband.

How does he know?

Well-known because of her association with men, she was already marked as "The" woman of Samaria. Blushing for the first time in a long time, Chava stammered with the new reverence of honest confession. "I have no husband."

Will he expose me to even more scorn?

He stood, a tall, sun-bronzed Galileean. Voice earnest but gentle, his reply revealed his own identity as he unmasked her secret. "You are right when you say you have no husband. The fact is, you have had five husbands, and the man you now have is not your husband. What you have just said is quite true."

They both knew it. Five relationships—two divorces, one desertion and two illicit liaisons--peppered her vermicular path.

Who are you? First a Jew, she thought, then sensing something more, she addressed him as "Sir." But now this gentle man could be one thing and one thing only.

"Sir, I can see that you are a prophet," Chava murmured, adding a bit defensively, "our fathers worshipped on this mountain." She jerked her head toward Gerizim. "But you Jews claim that the place where we must worship is in Yerushalayim."

It was a feeble rejoinder, but he had looked into her soul and she found his gaze unsettling. Penetrating. Probing. She gestured toward Mount Gerizim again, steep and rocky in the rippling heat of midday

"Believe me, woman, a time is coming when you will worship the Father neither on this mountain nor in Yerushalayim. You Samaritans worship what you do not know, for salvation is from the Jews. Yet a time is coming and has now come when the true worshipers will worship the Father in spirit and truth, for they are the kind of worshipers the Father seeks. Yahweh is spirit, and his worshipers must worship in sprit and in truth."

"I know that Mashiah is coming," she replied, evasive. "When he comes, he will explain everything to us."

How can this man know all about me and my life, and NOT be Mashiah? Could he be ...?

"I who speak to you am he."

Baskets bulging with lamb, lentils, figs and dates, Yeshua's disciples made their return. "Who is Yeshua talking to?" Yohannan queried, squinting into the sun as he wiped his dusty brow. Jaws dropped as they approached.

What is the master doing, talking with a woman in broad daylight, and a Samaritan woman at that?!

Chava knew. Leaving her water pot behind as a pledge of her return, she dashed into the city like a gazelle across the plain.

"Come, see a man who told me everything I ever did," she declared breathlessly to the men of the town, the men she knew only too well. Her countenance shone and while Chava did not presume to teach them, the same thought that had formed in her mind moments previously now sprouted wings in theirs and flew: *Could this be...?*

Woman. Samaritan. Sinner. Chava hadn't asked the young rabbi for anything. He did not grant any petition. No miracle was wrought except....?

Perhaps I am a... a... privileged woman! *He confessed to me that He was indeed the Mashiah, something He doesn't seem to have told even His disciples!*

... As far as the east is from the west, so far has he removed our transgressions from us.

Indeed. She had not sought Him; he sought out her.

Mashiah ...for Samaritans, too?!

~

"Her anxiety for her child has been exacerbated by the story of Herod's slaughter" Chuza confided to Hadessa later. He reproached himself constantly for telling his young wife the terrible truth. "Between the dreams, anxiety for the baby, and those accursed head swoons, she seems to be going mad."

Hadessa roundly chastised the steward of Herod Antipas for even mentioning the slaughter of the innocents. "How many times must I tell you that my `Hannah is fragile, delicate as a newly hatched chick? She never recovered after losing the babies, neither physically nor mentally. You must stop upsetting my lamb with such stories! No wonder her head hurts—it is but the reflection of her tortured heart!"

Yo-hannah's pounding migraine was the third in two days. Her suffering had not escaped the sharp, eagle eyes of the old woman. Hadessa snorted angrily before turning on her heel and stomping off to the kitchen where she banged pots and pans together and later laid out "a quick bite" suitable to feed Rome's legions. Meal preparations never failed to cool her ire, and Hadessa threw herself into the work, baking fresh bread and eggplant. Laying out hummus, almonds and bananas. Wine. Honey cakes and stuffed grape leaves.

Reclining at table later in a calmer frame of mind, Hadessa crunched a cluster of grapes and observed to a slightly pale Chuza, "My lamb is not going mad. She needs healing of heart and mind as well as body." The old woman paused, licking grape juice from her thick fingers. "I have no doubt that these attacks will stop when her soul finds peace and she is no longer afraid. Remember when the young carpenter rescued Rephaiah, the peace that flooded her?" Chuza nodded blandly. He was never quite sure what to say or how to respond to the old woman, who imperatives were often camouflaged as interrogatories.

Hadessa tossed the empty grape branch to a waiting servant, motioning for her to take it away. "Why, my lamb has given away half of her own treasury to support that Nazarene and his followers—out of gratitude, gratitude, do you hear?" Hadessa dabbed at her eyes. "Yeshua saved the boy at the seashore. But the mother needs a heart healing. Such fear," the old woman clucked, shaking her head sadly. "A young mother should not bear such a heavy load."

Chuza nodded his agreement. "Yes, yes. But who can heal a heart?" A man of high intelligence and ability, Chuza managed Herod's business matters and expenditures with a deft but capable hand. Heart-wholeness, however, was beyond his expertise.

"I can only think of one." Hadessa recalled a recent incident with a young man, perhaps thirty years old, tall, bearded, and extraordinarily ordinary.

~

But from everlasting to everlasting the Lord's love is with those who fear him, and his righteousness with their children's children.

~

Memories.

"Quick wife, the kerchief!" Veronica made a kerchief for herself and her husband. Inside the bundle were bread crumbs, representing their sins of the previous year. She and Yitzhak would join others at the foot of a high waterfall flowing from the springs of the Jordan River. The nearest sea was quite a distance away, and since the Jordan eventually wound its way into the Dead Sea, it was close enough:

You will again have compassion on us; you will tread our sins underfoot and hurl all our inequities into the depths of the sea.

Day of Atonement. *Yom Kippur*. The Shabbat of Shabbats. The rites would take up a whole day, beginning on *Yom Kippur Eve* or *Tishri 9*. On this most sacred of nights, the *Kol Nidre* service of "all vows" began the ten days of repentance.

The cantor would raise his voice in the familiar *Ashkenzai* melody, chant the prayer three times and ask God to annul all vows and oaths made during the past year that could not be fulfilled. The confession of sins, repeated several times during the day, enumerated only ethical lapses because only these, not crimes against fellow men, were atonable by performing the *Yom Kippur* ritual.

The service would end at sundown on *Tishri 10* with the closing prayer, *Neilah,* on the hopeful note that all who have repented have been inscribed into the Book of Life for the next year.

Yitzhak often murmured that the name was doubly appropriate "Because of the metaphorical tradition that the gates of heaven are open for repentance during the ten days preceding *Yom Kippur*." His eyes would twinkle, his face glow with anticipation. Finally, as the day ended, so the gates of Heaven closed and this special season for repentance was over. Yitzhak clapped his hands, "And then the fast ends with a feast!"

Veronica recalled the rich aroma of kebab—meat and vegetables on a skewer--falafel, pita bread filled with fried chickpea batter and salad, *shawarma* bread jammed with spit-roasted meat and cucumber. Her cook's *tshulnt* bean stew and *burekas* pastry filled with cheese and spinach made her mouth water. Then there was the Shabbat meal of soup, fish, and hearty *cholenta* stew. She preferred the hot, spicy baked fish of the Sephardim to the cold *gefilte* dish of baked or stewed ground fish served cold. Then there was vegetable salad mixed with olive oil and lemon juices. Ah, such a feast!

Veronica smiled faintly, fondly recalling Yitzhak's favorite song of this season: *I will praise you, O Lord, among the nations; I will sing of You among the peoples. For great is Your love, higher than the heavens; Your faithfulness reaches to the skies.*

The sun was setting, fizzing in the sky like a lazy melting medallion. The *hazzan* announced the start of Shabbat with three blasts from the synagogue roof. The first warned that Shabbat was imminent and gave a brief opportunity for people to finish their activities or a last minute task. The second indicated that housewives should light the Shabbat candles and say the blessing. From that moment, work must cease. The third blast proclaimed that Shabbat had begun.

Veronica dozed, remembering. She and Yitzhak began Shabbat every Friday evening lighting candles and reciting: *Blessed art Thou, O Lord our God, King of the Universe, who has sanctified us by His commands and hast commanded us to kindle the Shabbat lights.*

Yitzhak would pour the *Kiddush*, a blessing over a glass of wine which sanctified all joyous Jewish occasions. *Blessed art Thou, O Lord our God, King of the Universe, Creator of the fruit of the vine.*

Closing with the *Havdalah*, a ceremony separating the especially sacred day from the ordinary working days, Shabbat ended at sunset on Saturday. Together, Veronica and Yitzhak would recite the *Havdalah* at the close of Shabbat:

Blessed art Thou, O Lord our God, King of the Universe, who makest a distinction between holy and profane, between light and darkness, between Yisrael and the heathen nations, between the seventh day and the six working days. Blessed art Thou, O Lord, who makest a distinction between the holy and the profane.

~

Another woman loved the kaleidoscopic, vibrant feast where the skies dripped color and the people celebrated and danced. Living in a temporary shelter to remind them that even in the security of their own land, they were just as dependent on Yahweh for their needs now as their ancestors had been in the wilderness, Chava also loved the dancing, feasting, and laughing of the annual festival. Also the travel.

"Yes," she whispered, "the prophet Zechariah tells us of the time when the Lord is king over all the earth and the nations gather annually in Yerushalayim to keep the *Succoth.* Those who refuse to come are deprived of rain."

This feast points to Mashiah's rule of justice and peace in the world. When, O Adonai? When?

Inside the temple during *Succoth* the altar of sacrifice was decorated with willow branches. Processions of worshippers circuited the altar waving willow branches. Choirs of Levites sang antiphonal psalms to lyre, harp and reed flutes. "Hosanna," the people said, "O Lord, please save us."

Though he brings grief, he will show compassion, so great is his unfailing love.

The daily water libation ceremony during *Succoth* was really an enacted prayer for rain. The water libations reached a climax on the day of the Great Hosanna. Happy crowds surrounded the temple hoping to see the high priest as, in a procession of song and instrument, he wound his way down the steep hillside to the pool of Siloam. Dipping a golden flagon of about two pints' capacity into the pool, the high priest carried the water back up to the temple and poured it out at the base of the great altar. The trickle seemed so feeble, so inadequate.

Do I need but <u>a little</u>?

As if reading her thoughts, a voice suddenly cried out, "If anyone is thirsty, let him come to me and drink." It was a resonant baritone, strong and unwavering, rich in mercy and full of promise.

Chava started. *I know that voice.*

"Whoever believes in me, as the Scripture has said, streams of living water will flow from within him."

Blessed art Thou, O Lord God, King of the Universe, who hast sanctified us with His commandments and hast commanded us concerning the washing of... hands <u>only</u>?

Chava knew the voice and its owner without even looking. *I've heard that man before.*

~

This was once Veronica's favorite time of year. Usually falling in September or October, the observances began when autumn streaked the Judean hillsides with ochre, orange and saffron and the moon rose enormous and blood-red in the night sky. To the north near Caesarea Philippi, a crowded valley bursting with olive groves and vineyards receded into boulder-strewn foothills. Inky basaltic cliffs teetered over silver and green plane trees. Dewy tiaras crowned fertile fields and grasses. Farther up, a rich plateau of choice soil made a fecund bed for wheat and barley. The land lay fallow for now, resting until the fall rains arrived to settle the dust, after which planting and plowing would begin anew. It was already September. Not long to wait now.

Veronica remembered Yitzhak's twinkling eyes and mirthful voice. "Rosh Ha-shanah, a celebration for the new year and the creation of the world!" Yitzhak bubbled. He loved celebrations, especially those ushered in with the stout sounding of the *shofar*, the ram's horn.

"We must be solemn. This is no time for silliness!" Veronica would chide, knowing that the two-day observance was when she and her people were judged for their deeds of the past year. But she knew that her beloved husband was already looking forward to the next High Holy Day, *Yom Kippur*. Day of Atonement, four days before *Succoth*.

Succoth. The Feast of Tabernacles. A cornucopia of autumnal feasting, the occasion celebrated the completion of harvest and commemorated God's goodness to the people during the desert wanderings. Torah ordained rejoicing during this feast with willows, palms, fruit of goodly trees and leafy branches. How she loved the lively processions and the merry feasting!

A beautiful festival. Beautiful memories. So long ago. Before the illness. Before her own separation from The Holy.

Veronica had scarcely determined to head for Yerushalayim and her end when the High Holy Days were upon her. They came during Tishri, the first month of the Hebrew calendar.

AKELDAMA

At this time in his ministry Yeshua went around in Galilee, purposely avoiding Judea because the Jews there were bent on his death. He deflected urgings to head for Judea, where he could "show himself to the world." Yeshua declined saying, "The right time for me has not yet come."

~

Yom Kippur was the only day of the year when the high priest entered the inner sanctuary of the temple to offer sacrifice. The "ten days of repentance" would begin with New Year's Day. Symbolically loaded with the sins of the Jewish people, a goat would be driven into the desert to take away the people's sins.

Come now, let us reason together," says the Lord. "Though your sins be like scarlet, they shall be as white as snow; though they are red as crimson, they shall be like wool.

Veronica laughed a thin, brittle laugh at the Holy Day memory. *Wool? White? Snowy? Me*? The irony of the passage filled her mouth with a metallic aftertaste that set her teeth itching.

You have covered yourself with a cloud so that no prayer can get through...

She remembered the stories her maids whispered about the man from Galilee. About kindness, children, healings.

I have lost everything. It'll cost me little to find this Nazarene and see him for myself. What do they call him?

She couldn't recall his name, but Veronica pulled out a satchel and began piling food, clothing and other supplies inside. Her mind was made up.

If the young rabbi from Nazareth is going to Yerushalayim, then I am going there, too.

Thirty-one

Gaius kept his voice low, ever mindful of Herod's omnipresent spies who swarmed over the countryside like flies on a dead dog.

"By the time the tetrarch finished that wretched new city on the western hip of the Sea of Galilee, all he accomplished was offending those stiff-necked Jews!"

"Never mind that he named the place to honor the Emperor," hooted Julius, "I'd like to have seen the look on the tetrarch's face when they discovered that his model city was built smack on top of an old Jewish burial ground!" Both centurions knew that such a location would make the city unclean to the fastidious, religious Jews. No pious Jew would dwell there no matter how many splendid buildings Herod towered to the sky, monuments to his own megalomania.

"Still, it's quite a palace" Julius said, an amethyst breeze nipping his closely-cropped hair. They spoke of Herod Antipas' new residential palace in Tiberias, dutifully and garishly plastered with statues and graven images of various kinds.

"Sure, and that lunatic with the goat's hair tunic and wild beard roundly condemned Herod for the whole thing!" Gaius reflected, recalling how Yo-hannan had railed against Herod for such impiety in a capital city of a Jewish state. He watched his wife, Diana, swish up a silver arc of water and giggle beneath its downpour. She was soaked. Pretty lips puckered in a pout, Diana was beautiful but feather-headed.

The splashing retreated with a girlish giggle. The centurion's smile faded as Julius jerked his mind back to business with an inquiry about the new prophet from Galilee.

"What do you think of the man?" he asked, yawning in a manner that Gaius found suspiciously nonchalant. His bushy eyebrows creased like folds in a toga. Neither centurion knew what to make of the carpenter from Nazareth.

Nazareth is a non-place, a wide spot in the road. That dusty little village is a shoddy, corrupt midway stop between the port cities of Tyre and Sidon, overrun by Gentiles and Roman soldiers. Everyone knows Nazareth isn't much. How can anything good come from there?

"He seems harmless enough," Gaius opined. "This fellow isn't inciting riots or stoking coals for another Jewish uprising—at least, not yet."

"If so, it'll be the last thing he ever does in this province." Julius clutched his short sword with his right hand and made a slicing motion across his neck with his left. Both centurions fell silent for a stiff moment.

~

If I can just get near him, Veronica murmured, trembling. The press of the crowd was crushing now, and Veronica was as helpless as a grape in one of Yitzhak's wine presses. Jostled roughly by a stocky Idumean, she stopped and stared at the teacher's back. His hair was dark, his cloak a simple tan and green. Ceremonially unclean, Veronica could not bear to approach the young rabbi face to face. Worse, her uncleanness would be transmitted to anything—or anyone—she touched. But desperation knows no bounds. Her heart cried for his touch. Begged for him, pled to him.

If only he'd notice me. If he will just pause a moment and turn... if only...

The young carpenter was smiling, chuckling at a fisherman's joke hooked by the ham-handed Symeon, the irrepressible fisherman from Galilee.

AKELDAMA

The crowd pressed in on Veronica and she stopped, wobbly and weak. Veronica saw Yeshua, ten feet away. Now fifteen. Twenty. Her courage quailed as her legs turned to jelly. *What's the use? Haven't I sought a cure for this terrible illness for twelve years? How many doctors have come and gone, poking, probing, shaking their heads? What amount of fortune has been spent on their useless medicines, salves, concoctions? How near... how far...?*

~

The high priest was annoyed. Reports were flowing in from all Judea about a new religious crackpot, a leper-cleansing, health-restoring, lunch-augmenting, cripple-leaping self-styled "prophet" from Galilee who was "purifying" the unclean and "forgiving" sins! Some were calling him "mashiah."

This Galilean was a radical if Caiaphas had ever seen one. Worse, Yeshua's teachings threatened to disrupt the high priest's prim circle of order and the well-oiled political connections he had with Pontius Pilate and with Rome. Yosef ben Caiaphas stroked his beard thoughtfully, adjusting his phylacteries. He called for a scribe and papyrus and began dictating:

> *To: Pontius Pilate, Procurator of the Provinces of Judea, Samaria and Idumea.*
>
> *Your Eminence:*
>
> *I am writing to apprise Your Eminence about the Jewish concept of "mashiah" and how it may affect the government of this region. Out of concern for maintaining the Pax Romana which benefits us all, I endeavor to keep you fully informed of any likely appearance of such a "prophet" so that you may take whatever steps you deem necessary to address the situation sure to arise if the people should embrace such a so-called wonder-worker such as this new charlatan from Nazareth...*

Caiaphas paused thoughtfully, stroking his beard. *This Procurator is a Roman and therefore a pagan. What does he know of our beliefs? What does he know of our Jewish history, our culture and convictions?* The high priest peered down his beakish nose, cleared his throat and determined to enlighten the hand of Rome amongst the provinces.

> *Daniel predicted the appearance of a mashiah seventy weeks after Cyrus, the emperor of Persia, authorized the reconstruction of our temple in Yerushalayim. Rabbis have construed this prediction to mean weeks of years rather than weeks of days. That period of four hundred and ninety years expired just before King Herod was placed on his throne by Rome. Consequently, some very dangerous ideas are gaining acceptance among the Jewish people, ideas that may threaten us as well as the Pax Romana here.*
>
> *At this time, political events and natural phenomena are being analyzed by rabbis as to whether or not they relate to the prophecy of Daniel. I thought it my duty to tell you that most of these rabbinics, impractical scholars that they are, agree that the appearance of this foretold 'anointed one' is imminent.*
>
> *To wit: the birth of a savior is expected in accordance with the writings of another ancient author, Isaias, who wrote:*
>
>> For to us a child is born, to us a son is given, and the government will be on his shoulders. And he will be called Wonderful Counselor, Mighty God, Everlasting Father, Prince of Peace. Of the increase of his government and peace there will be no end. He will reign on David's throne and over his kingdom, establishing and upholding it with justice and righteousness from that time on and forever.
>
> *So it was into an ominous religious ferment that this rabble-rousing revolutionary named Yeshua was born.*

~

Just the hem of his garment... Adonai, King of the Universe, can you hear me? Will You heal me? I have no where else to go. Only to You.

Veronica was crawling. The press of the crowd knocked her

down again. On hands and knees Veronica approached him, head down, eyes tracing the ground. Fear clung to her like a mist. *What if he has no power? What if he cannot help me? What if he ignores me? Rejects me? What if....? Who are you?*

She approached Yeshua. There. His cloak, a little off his shoulder, brushing the ground on the right side. Almost there. So close… A heavy sandal trod on her hand.

His *simlah*, an over-robe worn as protection against the sun and during storms, draped over his left shoulder. And then she was within reach of the *tzitzit*, the tassel which rabbis wore on a *kethoneth*, a knee-length, wool tunic with half-sleeves.

Veronica saw the tassel, just out of reach, slung over Yeshua's back in such a way that the tassel of one corner hung between his shoulder blades. She stood.

Have mercy on me, O God, have mercy on me, for in You my soul takes refuge.

One teetering, tentative step. Another. *He who dwells in the shelter…* So close. *... of the Most High…*A heart's breath away. *... will rest in...* The crowd's forward movement suddenly picked up speed, hurrying ahead. Veronica quailed. Again. *… the shadow of the Almighty…*

Useless. Futile. I've been so foolish. Veronica turned to leave, to retreat back into the black hole of hopelessness that was her constant dwelling. She lacked both the speed and the strength to catch him. Her courage failed and she halted, sobbing quietly into her *keffiyah.*

I called on your name, *O Lord, from the depths of the pit. You heard my plea: Do not close your ears to my cry for relief.*

From twenty feet away there was a pause in Yeshua's pace. He did not turn, but he slowed and then stopped. He was engaged in conversation with two brothers, Yames and Yo-hannan.

Can you hear me, Merciful One? Are You listening, Giver of Grace?

The conversation continued and Veronica turned to go.

"Incurable" the physicians all said, pronouncing her condition beyond the skill of all medicine. She took a step back and some unknown force seemed to grip her, turn her shoulders with gentle hands and lead her, shaking, to the rabbi. *... He is my refuge and my fortress...*

Quivering, Veronica lifted her eyes and saw that the teacher had stopped. *... my God, in whom I trust.* The press of the throng was crushing, unwilling to make room for her. Veronica stumbled, regained her footing and continued forward on unsteady feet.

If I can just touch the fringe of his cloak... the hem near his feet... just a tassel... Fear flooded her throat, slid down her esophagus and emptied into her stomach. *How can I... ? I am unclean... I can't... Help me...* Veronica could not stop moving forward. *He will cover you with his feathers,...* One creeping, faltering step. *... and under his wings you will find refuge...* Then another. *... his faithfulness will be...*

Yeshua seemed to wait, hesitating in the dust. *... your shield and rampart.* His shadow fell on her. She was close enough to touch him.

~

Now let me see, where was I...? Caiaphas searched his beady brain as the scribe reviewed his dictation thus far. *Oh yes, the census.*

~

"So, what do you know of this Yeshua?" Nobai the Sadducee inquired testily of his servant. The high priest wasn't the only one who was uneasy with the growing popularity of a certain "prophet" from Galilee. The region simmered as a hot bed for revolt, which was why Nobai scattered his Herodian spies to comb the hills and vales of the Northern Province. They reported to him and he reported to "King" Herod Antipas, ever alert to potential uprisings and revolutionaries. This new "prophet" gave them all cause for pause.

"He has left Yerushalayim and headed north to Galilee, his home country" the servant replied as Nobai pressed his lips together in prim piety, drumming his fingers on a table.

"The man is no fool" the Sadducee muttered to no one in particular. "Yeshua obviously knows that Herod the Tetrarch will be more tolerant of a self-styled prophet than the Great Sanhedrin will be." The observation was undeniably true. "Keep an eye on him," the Sadducee snapped. He knew trouble when he saw it, and this "prophet" was full of it—in spades.

So the servant followed Yeshua to Galilee, where the rabbi's kind eyes swept the shores of the Sea of Galilee as he taught the crowds there. Every inch of soil around the sea was cultivated and the towns were thickly distributed, with densely populated villages. It was among these towns and villages, in this pleasant valley beside this lake, that Yeshua could be found. He shared jokes and laughter on the hills and in the fields, raced with children in small towns, but Yeshua stayed out of the new city of Tiberias, south of Gennesaret and Capernaum. It was Herod's winter resort on the western shore of the Sea of Galilee, where he resided with his venomous queen, Herodias, and her dancing daughter, Salome.

Aptly named for Herod's Roman benefactor, Tiberias groaned beneath the weight of graven images which adorned--defiled--most every structure. What is more, Tiberias hosted a mixed population, mostly Greeks and Syrians, because righteous Jews would not live in such a place, defiled as it was from being built atop an old Jewish burial ground. Add this to the beheading of his cousin by the tetrarch and Yeshua may have wanted to show his disapproval of this ungodly trio by staying far away from them. And he did.

Pondering this, Judah *ish keriot* once wondered aloud, "Why does the master avoid the larger cities, where his fame increases daily? These people are willing to sweep Yeshua into Yerushalayim like a king, right into and over Herod's own fortress!"

"Think about it, dumb bell," Thomas replied, punching Judah's shoulder, "why teach or minister in places with mixed inhabitants, towns that lack large Jewish populations? Teaching repentance and a new kingdom to Greeks and Syrians is like casting pearls before swine. Yeshua's message is for Jews only, is it not?" The other disciples grunted their agreement.

Thirty-two

"Who touched me?"

A number on a census slab, a babe in Bethlehem, a refugee to Egypt from the sword of King Herod, the Name with no name was now a grown man who felt a flow of power going out of him. Yeshua knew someone had touched him. His disciples peered at him quizzically. The majority of this band were fishermen and workmen from Galilee. Commoners. Not religious leaders, rabbis, nor experts in the law.

"What a silly question," big Symeon thought.

"The master is being jostled on all sides by the crowd," muttered Levi, "how can he say, 'Who touched me?'"

But the rabbi knew the difference between casual, accidental contact and the outreach of faith.

Veronica cowered, trying to escape notice, to be hidden. Legally unclean, she could not throw herself at his feet and state her complaint. Quivering in shame as she had these twelve long years of her affliction, Veronica soon saw that she was discovered. Trembling with self-consciousness, she confessed to her touch. "It was I."

Yeshua saw it in an instant. Soft brown eyes met hers. A smile of tender emotion tugged at his mouth. "Daughter," Yeshua said, eyes sparkling, "your saving faith has made you well." Redeemed. Spiritually and physically healed. "Go in peace."

For the first time in a dozen years, Veronica stood upright in a splash of Palestinian sunshine. No one could later recall that Yeshua addressed any other individual with the tender term, "Daughter." A true daughter of Avraham, Veronica found not her end but a new beginning as her faith was crowned by her Master. Reassured by Yeshua's kindness and tact, Veronica smiled, eyes streaming with grateful tears, "Praise be to the Lord, for He has heard my cry for mercy!"

The Lord is my strength and my shield; my heart trusts in Him, and I am helped. My heart leaps for joy and I will give thanks to Him in song.

Her Strength and Shield grinned as the Merciful One and a Mercy-ed one went their separate ways to a dual destination: Yerushalayim.

~

"They say Yeshua travels to Yerushalayim for the Passover!" Hadessa cried last week, clapping her hands. She was determined that her lamb would see this holy man, not from a distance or as one of a crowd, but up close. In person. Yeshua could heal her Hannah, if she could only get her there. But Yo-hannah refused to join her, not wanting to be separated from her son. She sent Hadessa on ahead.

"Secure our lodging. Make the necessary inquiries and preparations" the young mother said, pressing a bag of clinking coins into Hadessa's wrinkled hands. "We will meet you in the Holy City in a week."

~

Yeshua left Jericho with great crowds at his heels. Two blind men sat by the road. When they heard that Yeshua was going by they shouted, "Lord, Son of David, have mercy on us!"

"Oh no!" Andrew groaned, "We halt again. We have to get to Yerushalayim for Passover." His eyes scanned the dusty road, a half-day's journey through a treacherous canyon. "We can't stop now. Besides," he hissed to Levi, thumbing a digit at the two blind beggars. "Look at them!"

Most of the crowd avoided looking at "them." The blind duo was dirty, tattered and unkempt. Loud, obnoxious, pushy. Embarrassing. As vexing as a Negev grain of sand lodged under an eyelid.

"Can't they show more respect to the master?" Levi huffed under his breath, thinking, "We must have some proper procedures for this sort of thing. They should talk to Andrew first, then to Nathanael, then to me, and if their complaint seems important enough to carry it to the master, maybe I'll trouble him to stop a little further down the road, under some shade."

"Who do these beggars think they are?" Judah snorted. "They have no right to interfere with the master. He's on his way to the Holy City to set up his kingdom and deliver us from under the boot of Rome. The master has more important things to do than be bothered by these dirty beggars. Who has time for a couple of gutter snipes?" The crowd rebuked the sightless beggars and told them to be quiet, but they shouted all the louder, "Son of David, have mercy on us!"

"Son of David?" A title of Mashiah. Asking for what?

"Why do they ask for mercy, why not ask for their sight back?"

Somehow Yeshua heard them above the din, through the dust. He stopped and called to them, "What do you want me to do for you?"

"Isn't that obvious?" Nathanael said. "I mean, it's not as if they can see or anything!"

"Lord," they answered at the top of their lungs, "we want our sight." They were heard. Yeshua retraced his steps. Yeshua had compassion on them and touched their eyes. Immediately they received their sight and followed him.

Hadessa recalled the little drama as she shambled down the road. Her eyes were old but keen. She'd seen it all from a distance. Yeshua's touch of mercy. His ear attuned to the cry of the forgotten, the neglected, and the downtrodden stirred an ancient recollection.

Why did it seem that of all the eyes in that crowd, the blind were the only ones who really saw Yeshua?

~

"Anyone who has not seen the Yerushalayim Temple has not seen the glory of God" went the saying. It may have been true, as the "Herodian Temple" was indeed magnificent. As the Jewish historian Josephus would describe, the temple lacked nothing "that could astound either mind or eye. For, being covered on all sides with massive plates of gold, the sun was no sooner up than it radiated so fiery a flash that persons straining to look at it were compelled to avert their eyes, as from the solar rays. From a distance like a snow-clad mountain; for all that was not overlaid with gold was of purest white."

The temple—a shimmering splendor—housed the heartbeat of the Jewish faith and was set in Yerushalayim of Judea, the hub of leadership and orthodoxy. But Judeans were insular. They disliked rubbing shoulders with foreigners and had as little contact with them as possible.

Even so, pilgrims from the world over converged on the Holy City for the three annual feasts of Judaism. They swarmed over the land like ants after a sugar spill. The city also swarmed with all kinds of assorted crackpots and insurrectionists who invariably accompanied the pious at that time of year.

~

The old city stirred, stretching her spring arms. Indigo light melted into a citrus glow, heralding morning. Yerushalayim burst with song—chirping sparrows, burbling well water, children laughing, pottery clinking. It seemed an ordinary day. Gangs of workmen finished tidying up the roads leading into the old city. It was just after the winter rains, and the dirt tracks were rutted and uneven.

Tombs of holy men pockmarked the road on the other side. Though venerated, they still carried the contagious taint of corpse defilement. Workmen whitewashed the tombs to warn away the pious. *These tombs appear clean and attractive on the outside, but on the inside? Ugh!*

The crowds of travelers thickened as a withered old woman neared Yerushalayim. Trudging into the city for the high holy days on swollen, geriatric feet, Hadessa heaved her hulk onto the grass beneath the shade of an obliging quince tree. *What had the prophet Isaias written about this? Something about smoothing, straightening, banking up and preparing the highway that would precede the coming of Mashiah to Yerushalayim*?

Some miles from the city gate the ancient halted, huffing. A tall, dark woman peered at Hadessa from under thick eye lashes as she paused in her journey toward the city. The woman passed Hadessa, stopped a few paces ahead, and retraced her steps.

"I see, grandmother, that you have come a long way and are weary. I have extra wine and figs with me today," the dusky-haired woman with soft eyes spoke, "perhaps you would share some with me?"

The soft eyes spoke from a soft heart that matched a soft smile. Hadessa smiled back and agreed. Veronica shared her wine and her meal with a tired old woman. After eating, the two ladies shared the afternoon afoot, one with a newly healed and purified body, the other still searching.

~

Closing on the city with Veronica, Hadessa sniffed the air like a bloodhound after a scent. A memory stirred. A promise. There was something in the air. Something new. Something old. Crisp with expectancy, the early day held its breath, just as the bluing of a pre-dawn sky does before sunrise.

That was yesterday. The young woman who had shared her lunch and her kindness with Hadessa also shared her night's lodging at the home of an aunt. In gratitude, Hadessa invited her fellow traveler to celebrate Passover with her "soon to arrive" entourage. "I have gone ahead to prepare," Hadessa explained.

And so the two women agreed to travel together. It wasn't long before the duo met a lone, dusty woman who expertly massaged and bandaged Hadessa's weary legs and feet. She eventually warmed to their welcome. She was from Samaria.

The female duo became a trio. Like the expert haggler and handler she was, Hadessa secured Passover lodging for all in the old city and set about her next preparations.

~

The entourage approached Yerushalayim and came to Bethpage, the "house of figs," near the Mount of Olives. Just as the sleepy little town ambled into sight, Yeshua motioned to the village and bid his disciples to "find a donkey tied there, with her colt by her. Untie them and bring them to me." They did.

It was Sunday in Yerushalayim. Yeshua neared the city astride the gray animal as a large crowd spread their cloaks on the road before him, a mark of homage to the man who some now acclaimed as King.

Returning from an early morning foray into the *suk* with a bulging basket of fresh pomegranates, honey and matza flour and other food stuffs for the coming Passover, Hadessa noticed a young boy scampering down the street with a palm frond in hand. He was followed by another, then two more boys, a girl, and more. Curious, Hadessa halted and watched as a procession plodded down the road, apparently led by the young man on a donkey. *Such pomp and splendor! Who is the approaching royalty?*

Hadessa peered around a cart for a better look. Shouts rippled across thatched roofs, redounded off stone walls and echoed in the dusty streets: "Hosanna, Save now! Hosanna to the Son of David!"

Hosanna? "Son of David"? These terms are reserved for Mashiah.

The crowd surged through the eastern gate, also known as the "Golden Gate" or the "Gate of Mercy." It swept down into the valley of the brook Kidron, on through the groves of olive trees and upward onto the mountain to greet the man. Many carried palm fronds, holding them upright as if they were welcoming royalty. Others laid fronds across his path while some strewed their garments before him. Yeshua hardly paid any attention to them as he rode his donkey over their clothing like a long carpet that stretched down the hill before him to the stone bridge crossing the brook.

The boys outside the Damascus Gate at Yerushalayim played a game called *Basileus*, or *King*. They moved a wooden skittle, or bowling pin on the ground according to the throw of dice. When the skittle moved to the appropriate places for robing, crowning, and being given a scepter, the person who made the last throw shouted out, "King!" and collected the stakes laid out by his companions. Yeshua watched the game with an expressionless expression, neither mirthful nor forlorn, but somewhere in between.

The cries of the crowd hammered Hadessa's ears, "Blessed is he who comes in the name of the Lord!"

Who are you? Hadessa wondered, peering at the man on the donkey. She put down her basket and craned her neck for a better view. She caught a glimpse of the traveler as he rounded a bend and wet her lips.

He looks familiar. What is your name? Have I seen you before... ?

The rider had a tidily trimmed beard, dark hair of medium length cut above the shoulders, and the saddest eyes Hadessa had ever seen. Elbowing a bony old man for a wider view, a vague recognition stirred as she watched Yeshua approach.

A woman gripped a palm frond in front of Hadessa and yelled, "Haven't you heard? This is Yeshua, the prophet from Nazareth in Galilee. "

"But I thought he was a healer, not a king."

"Whatever he is, he can have the keys to the city today!" cried the woman, waving her palm frond like a fan.

I wanted to bring Yo-hannah here for a heart healing, Hadessa murmured. *Instead I find some new charlatan the people call a king.* She picked up her basket, shoulders sagging. *I have failed.*

~

Frond-like branches of cloud pricked the wild sapphire sky, spread like a canopy over the Holy City. Doves muttered in the trees. A spring breeze tugged playfully at noses and ears like a mischievous imp. The city hummed with excitement and anticipation. But there was more. A remembrance. A promise.

"This is what the Lord says," 'Restrain your voice from weeping and your eyes from tears, for your work will be rewarded,' declares the Lord. 'They will return from the land of the enemy. So there is hope for your future,' declares the Lord. 'Your children will return to their own land.'

Thirty-three

Greeted like an emperor by a madly rejoicing multitude, Yeshua and his processional set the high priest's teeth on edge. In truth, Yosef ben Caiaphas was outright alarmed, certain that the fellow intended to raise a rebellion against Rome.

Surely the Procurator will see the danger and act. I must finish my dictation to Pilate. Today. If he can't see the dangers of this religious charlatan and would-be king of his own accord, perhaps a few well-placed words may enlighten him.

Caiaphas re-read his review of Quirinius' census decree, Yosef and Miryam, unusual astronomical phenomena noticed by Babylonian astrologers and the Jewish concept of Mashiah. He continued:

> *... not much is known about Yeshua's growing up years other than an instance where he was lost at Yerushalayim and later found "teaching" in the temple, but we dismiss that report as pure folly. After all, Yeshua was hardly twelve years old at the time!*
>
> *Anyway, Miryam, the mother, and Yosef, supposed to be the father, took the child to Galilee. They returned to the town of Nazareth. In so doing, the couple seemed to be fulfilling in the child a prophecy that the mashiah would be called a Nazarene.*
>
> *For obvious reasons it is important that you, as governor of this province, should know all these things*

about the birth of this "prophet." I shall not exhaust your patience by telling you about his present doings, of which you are already quite well informed. But I do want to inform you that the traditions about the mashiah refer to his raising of the dead. A story is now being circulated about the carpenter resurrecting a man in Bethany. It's preposterous, of course, but remains a cause of great concern to me because of the prophecies, as it should be to you. After all, this is the same man who rode into Yerushalayim on a donkey yesterday. You saw the royal welcome the people gave him. I don't need to tell you how this man threatens our existence as a nation and as a people.

In your next report to Caesar please inform him that the high priests of Yisrael pray daily for his continued good health. I shall keep you informed.

With respect,

YbC

Ragged and dry, Caiaphas' voice slumped as he stopped dictating. The scribe re-read the letter. Caiaphas nodded his approval. Affixing his signet ring to the melted wax of the rolled scroll, Caiaphas bade the scribe deliver it to the governor with all haste. Swift-footed sandals raced out the door and down the street.

~

Pilate stayed in Yerushalayim during the week of Passover, as was customary. It was unseasonably hot and he considered going down to Caesarea, where delicious Mediterranean breezes cooled the stifling afternoons. *If only some of that cool air could be imported into this steaming cauldron and put a chill to some of this nationalist fire!* Pilate steamed as he performed his daily duties as governor in the Fortress Antonia, a great stone citadel less than a thousand yards from Herod's Yerushalayim palace.

We Romans tolerate odd, if not singular religious customs. It wasn't the solemn observance of the Passover rites that Pilate worried about, but the fact that the observances invariably brought hordes of Jewish pilgrims to "their" Yerushalayim from every corner of the Roman Empire.

Aren't there enough Jewish Zealots afoot, suicidal maniacs determined to drive their nation over a precipice in an attempt to throw off Roman rule? The Jews vehemently resented Roman domination while they fervently awaited their Mashiah, a king who would rescue them from Roman rule and restore their kingdom to them. The combination of Passover, pilgrims, and politics had to be handled carefully. Delicately. It was a task Pilate disliked but would undertake firmly and faithfully as a loyal subject of Rome. He sighed into the sweltering sky. *Isn't governing Judea difficult enough without these religious crackpots adding more fuel to the fire?*

~

"What is that?" Pilate bristled on the afternoon of the first day of Passover week. The sounds of singing and shouting in the street floated through this window. Pilate strode to a narrow window and looked out.

A tall man with dark hair was entering the city, riding on a gray donkey, a colt. His homespun robe was woven out of white wool, dyed brown with walnut juice. His hair was parted in the middle and fell to his shoulders, like most Jews. His eyes looked straight ahead as he rode down the street beneath Pilate's perch. The man's face, tanned and youngish, seemed solemn and serious.

Ever a quick assessor of character, Pilate noted that the rider carried himself with a calm, stately demeanor singularly devoid of the arrogance and sanctimonious vacuity common to so many of the hysterical, self-serving "prophets" he had witnessed during his rule in Palestine.

A throng lined the streets, swarming the rider and shouting, "This is the prophet Yeshua of Nazareth!" and "Blessed is he who comes in the name of the Lord!" Cries of "Hosanna! Hosanna!" fractured the air and echoed across the Kidron. A phalanx of dour, dark-robed religious leaders pressed against the street, demanding the rider stop such an outrageous display.

"I tell you," Yeshua replied, "if they keep quiet, the stones will cry out."

The scribes and Pharisees were in an uproar. "This Galilean has the audacity to call God 'my father,' a Mashianic claim! Do not the rabbis deduce from Scripture that Mashiah will be so close to God that only he will have the right to call Him 'my father?' Who does this man think he is?"

Just as Yeshua passed under Pilate's window, a messenger from Caiaphas appeared at the door, indicating in no uncertain terms that the high priest was "greatly agitated" with the ruckus in the street.

"Why should this display alarm your master? It is loud, but peaceful" Pilate countered.

"Because," the messenger explained breathlessly, gesturing out the window, "our prophet Zechariah wrote, 'Rejoice greatly, O Daughter of Zion! Shout, Daughter of Yerushalayim! See, your king comes to you, righteous and having salvation, gentle and riding on a donkey, on a colt, the foal of a donkey.'"

Pilate stroked his clean-shaven cheeks warily. His eyes narrowed into twin slits, roasting the messenger like red coals, "What about his appearance on the Mount of Olives?"

"That is where the Mashiah is supposed to appear. By doing that, this Nazarene is declaring to all Jews that he is Mashiah!"

Pilate paused a moment, then asked how "this rabble" had responded to Yeshua's appearance on the Mount just a day or two previously. The reply caused the furrows in his brow to deepen. Pilate had been mildly interested in the recent chain of events concerning this carpenter fellow, even amused. But this report indicated trouble.

The messenger gesticulated, "Caiaphas wants you to know what's happening. The high priest says this imposter wouldn't have ridden that donkey in from the Mount of Olives if he didn't intend to raise a rebellion! It means trouble!"

But he certainly didn't look like any king. He appeared to be near thirty years old. There was little in neither his clothing nor demeanor to denote royalty. *Besides, wouldn't a savior, their king, approach on a horse, a royal beast? Who was this man riding on a lowly donkey*? No Jewish king since Solomon had ridden upon a donkey officially.

Pilate hauled his meandering mind back to the meandering letter from Caiaphas. It included notes on a lengthy diatribe Yeshua had issued against the "Pharisees and hypocrites." He painted them as "whitewashed tombs, which look beautiful on the outside but on the inside are full of dead men's bones and everything unclean."

~

The crowd had just passed a *nefesh*, a pyramidal-shaped object considered a habitation of the soul of the deceased by Egyptian pagans, but regarded simply as a memorial among the Jews. The outside of the tomb had been whitewashed to denote a recent burial, thus warning Jews from contaminating contact with the dead. The implication was not lost on the crowd.

Yeshua wound up his scathing speech with a direct challenge to his enemies: "Woe to you, teachers of the law and Pharisees, you hypocrites!" Seeing the newly whited tomb in the distance, Yeshua's dark eyes raged as he chided the Pharisees, "Woe to you, teachers of the law and Pharisees, you hypocrites! You are like whitewashed tombs, which look beautiful on the outside but on the inside are full of dead men's bones and everything unclean."

~

If this Nazarene's mission is to infuriate and offend every religious leader from here to the Great Sea, I'd say he's doing a thorough job, Pilate observed over a goblet of fine Idumean wine. Pilate paused while his goblet was refilled. A warm breeze sputtered over the table candles, which a soft-soled servant leapt to re-light.

This man has the audacity of Octavian, if not the Emperor's political shrewdness. Pilate found himself grudgingly admiring the intrepid Nazarene. Thinking of how the high priest would respond to this latest turn of events, Pilate shook his head and chuckled.

~

A murmur rippled through the crowd. How can this Nazarene talk to the *Haverim* and *Hasidim* that way?

Undaunted, Yeshua continued, "In the same way, on the outside you appear to people as righteous but on the inside you are full of hypocrisy and wickedness."

Who is this? A wizened old woman wondered, listening. *He speaks like no other. He does not say, "God has spoken through me and therefore it will come to pass."* No. Hadessa had started to depart the throng, but something drew her back. Now she craned her neck to get a better look. *This Nazarene speaks with personal and absolute authority, as if... as if he was and is...* God! *No one has ever before dared to speak thus, but this Yeshua...?*

"You snakes! You brood of vipers!" Yeshua remonstrated. "How will you escape from being condemned to hell? Therefore I am sending you prophets and wise men and teachers. Some of them you will kill and crucify; others you will flog in your synagogues and pursue from town to town."

Jeremiah. Abel. Zechariah. The Valley of Hinnom. Punishment.

"O Yerushalayim, Yerushalayim," he sighed, shoulders quaking. "You who kill the prophets and stone those sent to you, how often I have longed to gather your children together, as a hen gathers her chicks under her wings, but you were not willing." Wide-set eyes swept the crowd, the same eyes that so often laughed and sparkled as though he knew something they didn't.

A broad breeze washed over Hadessa and receded like a gentle wave lapping the shore. Yeshua quietly continued, "Look, your house is left to you desolate. For I tell you, you will not see me again until you say, 'Blessed is he who comes in the name of the Lord.'"

The murmuring began.

What is he saying?

What does he mean?

Is he going away?

Shall we look for someone else?

Yeshua rounded and suddenly turned his gaze upon Hadessa. Those eyes. Such deep, sad eyes. Brimming with compassion, his twin almond orbs seemed to reflect all the suffering of the world.

~

Additional reports mentioned Yeshua's teaching on taxes, footstools, a widow's small copper coins, resurrection and marriage.

The latter seemed an odd subject to breach with a bunch of Sadducees, Pilate muttered. The Hand of Rome in Judea dropped his head and laced his fingers across his brow. He was suddenly tired. Very tired, indeed.

Thirty-four

Pontius Pilate dipped his fingers into the water basin. Stocky and squat, his falconish charcoal eyes were offset by a pendular Adam's apple, a crooked nose and sable hair, graying at the temples. The hard, thin mouth betrayed a tendency toward bigotry and obdurancy. He had a broad but angular face, without color, firm and resolute. Close scrutiny revealed a relentless expression which the unenlightened sometimes mistook for recklessness or sloth.

Physical appearance aside, none but a fool would mistake Pilate's ample girth or jowelled features for ineptitude or vapidity. His demeanor masked an alert, keen mind as lithe and agile as a big cat. A cold dignity clustered about the man, his feline cunning dripped with ambition.

Appointed governor of Judea, Samaria and Idumea by Lucius Aelius Sejanus, whom Tiberius Caesar had authorized to rule the Roman Empire on his behalf, Pilate pursed his lips and raked his hand through his hair. "These Jews are a millstone around my neck," he winced. "No people are more widely scattered throughout the Roman Empire than the Jews. Their businesses dot every seaport on the Great Sea. They reside in their own section of each town by choice, observe curious customs and worship their strange sole god in their plain temples—or, to use their word, *synagogues*. They have but one true temple. It is a gigantic monument in Jerusalem where hecatombs of animals are slain daily by their priests to propitiate their god." He mentally replayed yesterday's dinner conversation.

"These Jews, are they difficult to govern?" Pilate's visitor asked last night, voice slick as a well-oiled scythe.

"They can be," soured Pilate, stabbing a wayward slice of melon with his index finger. "They are self-righteous and offend everyone with their endless insistence that their god is the only real deity. Can you imagine that?" Melon juice trickled from the corners of his mouth. "Worshipping one god, and one god only?"

They ate reclining at a *triclinium*, an arrangement of three tables set around a square. Access to the middle was gained through the open side of the square so that servants could come and go to bring in food and remove leftovers. Lucius had already polished off the *gustatio* appetizers of bread and cheese and was gulping down the multi-course *cena* with the ravenous rush of a wolf. Pilate rolled his eyes at his nephew's table manners while a servant refilled his wine goblet.

"Think of it, Lucius: Greeks, Babylonians, Egyptians, everyone tolerates everyone else's religion, as civilized people should. We Romans top them all, naturally. We accept and worship any deity that appeals to us. We are willing to pay appropriate deference to the god of the Jews, but these Jews treat our gods with contempt, refusing to acknowledge them in any way. Worse, they vehemently express denials of the divinity of the emperor, a dangerous practice which has made them subjects of questionable loyalty ever since Caesar Augustus was recognized as a god almost a hundred years ago."

"I hear they worship Bacchus in secret," Lucius wheezed. Pilate rarely looked forward to his sickly nephew's visits. The young man was thin, slovenly, and ravenous. *He eats like a Roman legionary.* Still, the Judean heat seemed to agree with the younger man's frail lungs, so Pilate grudgingly indulged his sister's annual request and braced himself for Lucius' inevitable arrival each spring.

How anyone so "sickly" can eat like a common camel drover, I will never understand, Pilate muttered to himself. Lucius had long since drained the meal's "starter" of wine diluted with honey. The main dinner, the *cena*, included three courses of succulent roast lamb, broiled chicken, and shellfish. Each dish arrived in the hands of a servant on a lacquered tray, beautifully decorated.

"You have been misinformed, my gullible young relative." Pontius wiped his hands on fresh linen as he exploited the opportunity to display his expertise on the subject in question. "That misnomer has arisen out of a misunderstanding regarding the great golden grapevine that adorns the exterior of the Jewish temple in Jerusalem."

"So, what of this Jewish god, this so-called 'one god' they claim?"

"The god of the Jews is a mysterious one, invisible and omnipotent. They think of him as the creator of this world and the father of mankind. They believe he is present in the most holy part of their temple in Jerusalem."

"The monstrosity that Herod built?" Lucius looked around for the *mensae secundae,* hoping for pastry and fruit. Bouquets of jasmine, roses and lilies scented the night air. A parrot squawked. A slave held out a morsel to the noisy bird, which swished for it in a flutter of emerald and scarlet. *I will make him wait for dessert until this lesson is complete*, Pilate decided, reaching for another pickled egg.

"Yes, inside the temple where their one god supposedly dwells is a windowless room behind a great curtain. It's a dark vault where no one but the high priest can enter, and he may only do so on the most holy day of the year. Pompey entered that huge cubicle by right of conquest and found it to be peculiarly empty." Pilate's tone turned tinny. "He intended to seize their god and haul it back to Rome, to hold it hostage in return for their good behavior. But there was no god to be seen and worshipped in that enormous place. It was empty, do you hear me, empty!" Lucius still contemplated pastry and grapes sweetened with honey. He nodded vaguely, eyes vacant.

"Another belief of the Jews relates to Palestine," Pilate lectured. He knew a good deal more about these Jews than he let on. "The Palestinian land was supposedly promised to the Jews by their god, according to one of their ancients. It seems rather odd that they can convince themselves their god thinks so much of them. Wouldn't a god who truly cared for his people have given them a richer, more fertile land than this chunk of dust? Wouldn't he have given them some land other than one in the path of every conquering army that rampages through it, leaving desolation in its wake? Even so, Jews think it contrary to the will of their god that any Gentile should possess one square foot of this miserable, arid land."

Pilate clapped his hands and slaves and parrot scurried away, returning moments later with silver trays heaped with honeyed raisins, dates and nuts folded inside a double pastry crust. Stuffing another dessert into his swarthy mouth, Lucius turned a suddenly attentive face to his noble—if not prosaic—uncle.

"Their religion is based on five books attributed to Moses," the governor continued, "as well as on the ancient writings of other religious mystics. Most of those other authorities predict the eventual coming of a savior of the Jewish people. In their language he is called 'Mashiah.'"

"Mashiah?"

"Yes, Mashiah."

Lucius nibbled the Jewish word, sampled it, gnawed it, tasted it. Rolled it around on his tongue. *A strange word* he finally decided, *with a decidedly displeasing taste*. "What does it mean?"

"It means 'anointed one.' In Greek, 'mashiah' becomes 'christ.'"

"Just what, exactly, is this so-called 'mashiah-christ' supposed to do for these wandering nomads?"

"Well, the Jews say he is a leader who will come and deliver them from foreign oppressors and then reign in Jerusalem not only over Jews but over everyone," he snorted, "the world over, in an empire that will be eternal."

Lucius stiffened. He knew the word "mashiah" had an acetous flavor. "That's quite a concept for a minor nation that has been ground under the heel of one foreign conqueror after another for the last thousand years! By the way, this mashiah of theirs, does he have a name?"

"None that I know of, and as far as the 'concept' is concerned,

Jewish delusions of grandeur come and go like the seasons." Pilate yawned, musing moodily that the arrival of Lucius' *sedom*, his two-horse carriage which was to transport him home, couldn't come soon enough. "But they can plant and harvest a bushel of 'mashiahs' for all I care, so long as I don't have to quell any more revolts and thus retain the favor of Rome."

~

It was early spring. Clear light dappled the valleys and tiptoed across the plain of Jezreel. Reports continued to arrive that Yeshua was telling his disciples that he would die on a cross in Yerushalayim.

Pullulating with pilgrims from all parts of the Middle East, Yerushalayim became a veritable powder keg of religious fervor and anti-Roman sentiment during these holy weeks. Pilate found it politically expedient—if not personally discomforting—to remain in the old city during these curious Jewish festivals.

His spies and messengers brought in all sorts of stories about the carpenter as the week progressed. Odd reports dribbled in: Yeshua cursing a barren fig tree, Yeshua shouting at merchants and money changers at the temple about his house being a house of prayer, not a den of thieves.

"Curious one, that" Pilate remarked. He had often seen the pilgrims buy their sacrificial animals from the flocks reared by the temple authorities. If pilgrims brought their own animal, there was no guarantee that the examiners would pass it for temple use. It seems that they frequently declared an animal "unfit" for sacrifice on the grounds of some blemish which its owner was not qualified to challenge, thus forcing him to buy from the temple flocks.

Pilate noted those who "sat at table" in the outer court of the temple, marked as moneychangers by the silver half-shekel they wore in the ear. Such persons rendered a service useful to worshipers coming to pay their temple tax or purchase their sacrifice, and for that service the moneychangers exacted a fee, traditionally one twenty-fourth of a shekel. With worshipers thronging the city from many regions, the moneychangers not only changed local coins into various denominations but also changed foreign coins into local currency. Thus, Jews far and wide could pay the half-shekel temple tax required of them.

Pilate had been told that these moneychangers, though despised by the Jews, actually offered an important service to their surly customers. All portraiture was considered a profanation to pious Jews as a violation of the Torah commandment against graven images. Further, some of the emperors looked upon themselves as divine and had themselves or members of their family depicted as gods or goddesses on their coins! The pious Jew, though forced to use the hated Roman coinage, would at least be able to exchange Roman coins for coins without portraiture or reference to pagan gods. With that "purer" money he would then buy a sacrificial animal.

And so the temple money changing business kept humming as pilgrims had to exchange their ordinary money for the temple coinage to avoid using Roman coins and to buy an acceptable "unblemished" animal to sacrifice. Festivals were peak trading times and the temple till was certainly not left wanting, a practice that seemed to infuriate the young carpenter. Both reports were filed by Pilate's operatives on Monday.

~

"By what authority are you doing these things? Who gave you this authority?"

Yeshua replied with questions and stories—questions about Yo -hannan—"was his baptism from heaven, or from men?" He seemed to challenge the Jewish religious leaders at every opportunity. There was more. Stories about landowners, a vineyard and evil tenants who murdered the landowner's son to get his inheritance.

"He must have a point" Pilate muttered over the reports. "What is it?"

~

AKELDAMA

A sweaty messenger arrived for the Procurator. Pilate glanced up from his desk. *What's this? Another hysterical epistle from Caiaphas?* Pilate received the scroll, dismissed the boy with a distracted wave of his hand, and opened the parchment. Caiaphas' report was full of reports about "that infamous Nazarene" – rumors of miracles, charges of heresy, associations with publicans and tax collectors, eating with unwashed hands. Curing a paralytic and telling him his sins were forgiven. Pilate could've cared less about these matters. They were religious affronts and of no interest to Rome. Caiaphas wrapped up his usual long-winded letter with:

> *... The aforementioned reports and others have left me to draw only one conclusion about this Yeshua: he is an apostate of the worst possible sort. Mark my words, Eminence, it won't be long until this Yeshua stirs up another populist revolt. Indubitably, Yeshua means trouble for both of us. I shall continue my surveillance of his activities and keep you informed.*

This was something different. Revolts interested Pilate because they interested Rome. There were other reports besides those from Caiaphas. Reports filtered in from all over indicating that this Nazarene bore strict scrutiny. Strict scrutiny, indeed.

Thirty-five

Each day of the past week Yeshua did or said something to appall and otherwise insult some element of the Jewish religious cadres. The chief priests now met in the palace of Caiaphas to discuss how they might take the Nazarene by stealth in some private place. Yeshua's support among a substantial minority of the populace remained strong, so they did not want to arrest him in public as Jewish law required. That might result in disorder and bloodshed, and he might escape in the ensuing confusion. Neither option looked good. Nor did Caiaphas' latest simpering letter to the governor, some nonsense about raising a friend back to life in Bethany.

But Yeshua's popularity among the people grew daily. Alarmed, Caiaphas gathered the chief priests in his palace. "What shall we do?" he asked, "this man seems to work miracles. If we ignore him, leave him alone, everyone will think he is the Mashiah. Then the Romans will come in, take away our lands, disperse our people, and destroy our nation."

Like Annas his father-in-law, Caiaphas was a Sadduccee. His policy was compromise with Rome and manipulation to get his way. But the Pharisees were the prevailing party among the Jews. They followed no particular profession and could be scribes, fisherman, merchants, doctors, bankers, farmers, or cobblers. Pharisees were the party of the rabbis who are scholars and students of the scriptures, interpreters of the law.

In spite of their commanding influence upon Jewish religious thought, the Pharisees numbered barely six thousand. They were concerned about Yeshua for spiritual reasons, but Caiaphas' main concern lay elsewhere. As high priest of the Jews, he was Pilate's appointee. The governor needed the high priest to keep the Jews in line; the high priest needed the governor's favor to retain his position.

"The Jews may not like it," Pilate observed acidly, "but having the governor appoint the high priest is advantageous to Rome, which is advantageous to me." He knew that the term of office was but one year, making it easy for governors to keep the spiritual leader of the Jews on a short leash. Caiaphas always supported Pilate, Pilate's projects and Pilate's politics; his annual reappointment was a given.

"It is expedient that one man should die for the people, that the nation not perish," Caiaphas now proclaimed to the council. The priests and elders thus congregated agreed that Yeshua should be put to death. They issued a decree that any person knowing the location of the carpenter must reveal it so that Yeshua could be placed under arrest.

"What are you willing to give me if I hand him over to you?" one of Yeshua's twelve closest followers asked the chief priests. Delighted with the offer and ensuing plan, the priests counted out thirty silver coins. From then on Judah watched for an opportunity to hand Yeshua over to them, perhaps after the night's Passover celebration?

~

The big fisherman continued in a low voice later, "Thursday was a long day. We had recently come from Bethany," he motioned toward the southeastern hip of the Mount of Olives rising just to the east of Yerushalayim. "We walked all day. Even my teeth were tired."

"After eating Passover, Yeshua, Yames, Yo-hannan and I went out the eastern gate of the city and across the brook Kidron. It was nearly midnight when we walked out of Yerushalayim, passed through the valley and climbed the path to an olive orchard on the nearest slope of the Mount of Olives and a quincunx of trees. Yeshua was weary, heavy-laden. He rested against an olive press there. Then the teacher said, 'My soul is overwhelmed with sorrow to the point of death. Stay here and keep watch with me.' He fell to the ground, crying out something about a cup, a chalice of death and wrath."

"To whom did he cry out?" Yo-hannah prodded. Each time her eyes caressed Rephaiah, Yo-hannah's heart swelled with gratitude and she provided Yeshua money from her own purse. She, Chuza, their son and some servants were newly arrived in the royal city to meet Hadessa for Passover. But what happened last night? What happened on Thursday night and early Friday?

Chuza had taken Rephaiah to the home of a cousin, ostensibly to play. In reality, both mother and father had thought it prudent to shield the boy from the harsh words and impending violence that seemed to hang in the air like soot. Yo-hannah felt the blackness seep into her bones, pound inside her head. And where was Yeshua? He had vanished overnight. Surely something was amiss. Yo-hannah had to know, hence her intense questioning of Yeshua's followers: "To whom did Yeshua cry out? On what name did he call?"

Yo-hannan stared at the lady quizzically, picking his raw mind. "He said, 'Abba, Father, everything is possible for you. Take this cup from me. Yet not what I will, but what you will.'"

Abba? Yo-hannah's usually nimble mind fused. Not *El Shaddai*, God Almighty? Not *El Elyon*, God Most High? *El Olam*, God the Everlasting? Or *Elohim*, Strong and Mighty One? These names of God she understood, but *Abba*? Her eyes blazed, her face flushed. How could anyone dare address the *Adonai Elohim*, Lord God, King of the Universe, with such familiarity, such intimacy?

A desperate scene at the sea fluttered through Yo-hannah's memory. *You told us your name, how you must long to be close to us. As close as a ... **Daddy? Papa?***

"We didn't mean to fall asleep while the master prayed," Yo-hannan protested, rubbing red eyes, "but next thing I knew, Symeon, recently renamed Petros, was snoring and so was Yames."

Yo-hannan's eyes poised on a particularly interesting slice of ground at his feet, which he studied intently. "I guess I nodded off, too."

Gnarled trees with hollow trunks. Sleeping friends. What must be done, only he could do. While Yeshua's followers snored, a cosmic conflict raged. Yeshua entered the supreme struggle alone, and a moonlit olive grove became a battle ground. At the end, Yeshua accepted the *Abba* answer and made his decision: crimson victory among the olive trees.

"Next thing we knew," Petros mumbled,"*Ish-keriot* and a whole crowd arrived armed with swords and clubs, sent from the chief priests and the elders of the people. Then *Ish-keriot* kissed Yeshua. Men stepped forward and seized him like a common criminal!"

A Judah kiss. A snake's hiss?

Petros' eyes filled, recalling a cock's crow. He paused for a cryogenic moment and then exploded into speech. Yo-hannah learned three new words as well as several unusual uses for respectable words that would never have occurred to her. The rough, raw-boned Galilean looked around as if dazed, took in Yo-hannah's flushed cheeks and shut his mouth with a snap, saying, "Sorry, lady. I forgot to remember myself." Yo-hannah accepted Petros' apology and the big fisherman buried his head in his hands, choking back huge chunks of dual shame.

"Then what?" Yo-hannah turned gently to Yames. The events of the past week made her head spin, especially last night. The wife of Herod's steward asked the question even as she dreaded hearing the response.

Yames stared at the ground, chin on his chest. Voice barely audible, he whispered, "We ran. All of us. Scattered like sheep without a shepherd."

~

Midnight melted. Darkness overflowed the land with astonishing speed. The blue-black sky was so sprinkled with stars that it seemed a mist of light floated on the umber mountains, with their immense silence made up of a thousand tiny sounds and the intoxicating scent of warm earth and wild plants. A jubilant green tapestry unfurled over the hills, embroidered with tulips, wild gladioli, warm yellow crocuses, blood-red anemones, and dawn.

~

The hammering of desperate fists on the door of Caiaphas' palace crashed into daybreak. One of Yeshua's followers, a haggard-looking fellow, was beating a tune on the door like a drum. When the priest opened the door, Judah *ish keriot* withdrew a money bag from his tunic. He extended the bag toward the priest. Both Judah and the priest knew the contents of that coarse skin bag: thirty pieces of silver. Blood money. Money he had been paid for betraying his master. Apparently overcome with remorse or shame, maybe both, the disheveled disciple thrust the money bag at the priest wailing, "I have sinned, for I have betrayed innocent blood!"

"That is your problem," the priest replied gruffly, slamming the door in his face. Judah cried out in dismay and went up to the temple, where he cast the silver through the gate onto the stone floor. The priests picked up the coins and said, "It is against the law to put this into the treasury, since it is blood money." They decided to use it to buy the potter's field as a burial place for foreigners.

Akeldama. Field of Blood. Valley of Ben Hinnom. Valley of Slaughter. A place of sacrifice. Fireplace. Trash dump. *Gehenna.* The potter's field. Thirty pieces of silver. The bargain for betrayal.

Thirty-six

Pilate's lithe mind recounted recent events as a practiced eye scans a scroll. First the carpenter had ridden into the old city on a humble gray donkey, with a pomp and splendor that would have pleased Tiberius Caesar himself. *Pressing his luck, he is, or maybe this 'teacher-prophet' is on a suicide mission?* Pilate's mind paged back to the third and fourth days of the past week when Yeshua had publicly insulted the scribes, Pharisees and Sadducees. *Then there's that business about my wife's dream. What can be made of that?* Procula shifted restlessly in her brightly dyed *stola* as she related a dark dream fraught with warning about this curious carpenter.

This Yeshua can't seem to go anywhere or say anything these days without enraging someone. Pilate knew the feeling all too well. He himself traversed a hair-fine line as he attempted to balance politics, religious riots, a sullen local populace, loyalty to Rome, and bitter political enemies who would like nothing better than to see the governor tossed off Tarepian Rock.

~

"The Sanhedrin has spoken," Pilate pronounced crisply. "A court made up of priests and elders and rabbis should only be allowed to act as a religious tribunal, which they have. It was right for Caesar Augustus to deprive the Great Sanhedrin of the authority to hear civil and criminal cases. It was also right to deprive those self-righteous hypocrites of the power to inflict the death penalty."

"They can still find a man guilty of heresy and stone him," Gaius returned edgily. Nearly four months into his Judean posting, the centurion quickly became Pilate's top aide and military advisor.

"Yes, but not without my approval," countered Pilate.

"The carpenter has been saying he is the son of their god" Gaius replied. "The Sadducees want to get rid of him."

"Of course. They'll arrest him and try him if he doesn't depart the city."

"Yes, but they won't want to try him. There are thousands of Jews here to celebrate Passover, and it's possible that the carpenter has more support than the priests have. If that's true, the effect upon the priests could be devastating. They will want to eliminate the carpenter swiftly."

Pilate grunted. As the governor mentally reviewed the events of the past few hours, he realized that what this centurion said about the Jews and their Sanhedrin had transpired precisely as Gaius predicted. This realization only added to Pilate's annoyance with this whole Yeshua business.

"So?" Pilate's tone could have crushed granite.

"Well, it takes time to do what has to be done before a man can be put on trial as an apostate before the Council of Seventy. I'm told they expect to take Yeshua prisoner tonight, and they'll want to be rid of that fellow as soon as possible."

"Fine. But why should I care?"

"Because," Gaius explained, struggling to hide his frustration with this vapid governor, "they will want to have him tried, condemned and executed tomorrow. They can't try a man on the day before the Shabbat even if they could get the court together, because their law provides that a guilty verdict cannot be rendered on the same day as the trial. And executions are prohibited on the Sabbath."

"What's that to me?" Pilate snapped in a serrated voice.

"There are a lot of other complications. An apostate must be condemned by a lower court before he can be prosecuted before the Great Sanhedrin. The priests want to avoid that. They believe the carpenter is a false prophet and intends to lead a rebellion."

Ah. "Rebellion" was a well-known word in the governor's political lexicon, one he smashed in an instant. Gaius saw Pilate's visage darken into purple.

"It would be many days before Yeshua could be condemned to death as a heretic, perhaps perilous days," the centurion's voice fell thickly on the last three words. Pilate did not miss the implication.

"So?" the governor replied tartly, pacing his marble portico.

"They are going to bring him to you tomorrow and ask you to crucify him." Verbalizing what should have been obvious a week ago, Gaius saluted his superior. The centurion had a bad feeling about this Nazarene, ever since the night his former armor bearer appeared to him in a dream, nattering on about that "unknown, loving God" nonsense.

How can anyone "know" an Unknown? Why, to make himself known to man, this god of Arieh's would have to condescend to the level of man, accommodate himself to limited, finite consciousness! Would Arieh's 'Unknown god' reveal himself to us in the flesh, tread our dirty roads, eat our food and speak in human language? Outrageous! Unthinkable!

Even so, Gaius hadn't slept since his encounter with the Nazarene. He was near Capernaum, conferring with a fellow centurion. Usually pin-prick precise, Justinian seemed distracted that day, vague. Gaius learned that the man's favorite servant was ill, hovering close to death. He'd paid a fortune for the lad, but the relationship resembled that of father and son more than master and servant. So when the boy fell ill with the brain fever, Justinian despaired for his life until he heard of Yeshua. Justinian sent some elders of the Jews to Yeshua, asking him to come and heal his servant. As the Nazarene neared Justinian's house, the centurion sent friends saying, "Lord, don't trouble yourself, for I do not deserve to have you come under my roof."

"Hmph!" Gaius muttered. *A Roman soldier groveling to a Jew? Justinian has gone soft. Why, even these Jews seem to admire the man. What's the matter with him?*

"That is why I did not even consider myself worthy to come to you," Justinian continued. "But say the word, and my servant will be healed."

What in the world..?

"For I myself am a man under authority, with soldiers under me. I tell this one, 'Go,' and he goes; and that one, 'Come,' and he comes."

"This I've got to see" Gaius grunted. He did. Gaius hadn't slept since. Tonight would be no different.

Pilate waved the centurion away distractedly, and Gaius departed for the nearest tavern as swiftly as his steed could carry him.

~

Dawn blinked her Friday eyes as a blush of rose splashed the Yerushalayim hills. Rumors filled the streets like rain in a bucket with the uneasy arrival of morning.

"They took him to the High Priest's palace last night and tried him for creating a disturbance in the temple, defiling it."

"Defiling *what?"* an observer laughed derisively. "As if anyone could 'defile' a temple that's already been turned into a stable and a den of thieves!"

"They had enough people on their side to convict him though, didn't they?"

"Yes, I heard they rushed Yeshua over to the Insula and got the Procurator out of bed to hear the case."

"What did Pilate do?"

"He told them to settle it amongst themselves, like it was just another temple free-for-all. The chief priests were as angry as a kicked hornet's nest!"

"I bet they were! Did they let Pilate off with that?"

"Of course not! They claimed that Yeshua was trying to make himself a king. Pilate didn't swallow that, but he was in a tight spot. He needs the Sadducees to keep peace with the people."

"Yes, and save his own hide!"

"Then someone shouted, 'Kill the Galilean!' Well, you should've seen old Pilate's ears prick up at that! 'If this man is a Galilean,' Pilate said—as if he didn't know--'then he should be tried before Herod. He's the tetrarch of that region and handles all Galilean matters.'"

"And...?"

"The guard fell in around the prisoner and dragged him up the street to the old Hasmonean palace and Herod. That old buzzard didn't seem to know what to do with the Nazarene, either. He questioned Yeshua, but the prisoner made no answer. So Herod ordered Yeshua lashed again. Some drunken lout dredged up purple regalia and put it on Yeshua, pretended to bow down to him. Another one slammed a crown of Yerushalayim thorns on his head. Eventually, Herod ordered the soldiers to return Yeshua to Pilate. Even then, those old crows weren't satisfied. They want Yeshua dead."

"Put to death?"

"Yes, but only Pilate can give that order. So they all went back to the Insula."

"They're at the Insula, now?" Gaius croaked. The narrator nodded. Gaius' mind reeled from an overabundance of last night's wine. The lazy afternoons munching dates and figs on the river bank with Julius and their wives were gone, passing into the musty history of four months' past when his new orders arrived. Now the centurion leapt into his saddle and dashed down the streets to the Praetorium.

Thirty-seven

Pilate was clearly uneasy with the young Jew who stood bound and bloodied in his courtyard. The carpenter from Galilee had been held all night in the palace basement of Yosef ben Caiaphas, chief of the Great Sanhedrin of Yerushalayim, until the prisoner could be brought before Pilate in the morning.

The governor stood within the colonnade, surrounded by a phalanx of sullen palace guards, tightly packed and briskly attentive. He donned his toga *praetexta*, the special toga purfled by a purple stripe indicting his position as magistrate. A company of troops cordoned off the highest level of the terraced flagging, the *lithostrotos,* the court of the Antonia fortress, where Pilate set up his Praetorium. Before them stood the captive, alone.

The crowd was thick and boisterous. Tension rippled through the throng like ocean waves battering a beach. Yeshua wore the crown of thorns as reported. His hands were bound. Blood ran down his brow and face. His clothing flapped loosely, revealing livid welts and slashes from the whip, some still bleeding. Yeshua did not seem conscious of his injuries and the Procurator's interrogation proceeded quietly as the prisoner responded in a confident but respectful tone.

"He says he is our king!" one of the priests shouted. "We are charging him with sedition. You must try him on that charge."

The Procurator asked Yeshua about his identity, kingship, and truth. He couldn't shake the impression that, despite appearances to the contrary, everyone on this flag-stoned courtyard was on trial *except* the carpenter.

Flustered, Pilate offered to release another prisoner instead of Yeshua, as was his custom during Passover Week. Stone-eyed and flint-faced, the hostility of the influential crowd bubbled up and overflowed its bank like an oozy alkaline spring, poisoning all.

"Crucify him! Crucify him!" the crowd roared.

"Why?" Pilate countered, "What evil has he done?"

"Crucify him!" they chanted.

In hopes of mitigating their hostility toward the carpenter, Pilate turned to Gaius and ordered Yeshua scourged. Gaius ordered the man's purple robe removed, the robe in which Herod had sent Yeshua back to Pilate. Another soldier took Yeshua's homespun robe. Gaius exited the room and returned momentarily, handing a junior officer a metal-tipped scourge. The soldier laid it across Yeshua's back with gusto as two other soldiers held the prisoner's arms. By the time he was done, the soldier's arm and shoulder ached, but Yeshua's back and shoulders were a bloody pulp.

But he was pierced for our transgressions, he was crushed for our iniquities...

It wasn't enough. The soldiers brought Yeshua into the hall again, dragging him before his accusers. Pilate raised one hand and pointed, "Behold the man."

A chorus of "crucify him!" slammed against walls and pillars.

"You crucify him," Pilate said. "I find no fault in him."

It was true. The Sanhedrin charged Yeshua with blasphemy in that he called himself the Son of God, a term used in an official or mashianic sense signifying God's heir and representative. Such an indictment involved the religious sentiments of the Jews and thus carried no weight with a Roman governor. So the charges were changed from religious to political.

If I was convinced that these charges were true, I would not hesitate for one instant to condemn this carpenter character to death, Pilate contemplated silently. But he suspected the accusations were false. After interviewing Yeshua at his palace,

Pilate was even more firmly convinced that this carpenter was completely innocent of any treachery toward or rebellion against Rome.

"Yeshua admitted that he is 'King of the Jews,' whatever that means," Pilate muttered. "But he went out of his way to convince me that his kingdom was a spiritual one, not of this world." Pilate shifted uneasily on a seat that had suddenly become a knife's edge.

Can it be envy that's motivating the Jewish authorities to hand this man over to judgment? Pilate's position was a thorny one. He knew very well that the accused was innocent and he pronounced him thus, but at the same time Pilate realized that the Jewish leaders were determined to procure a death sentence for the carpenter. He could evade responsibility by sending Yeshua to Herod on the palm -frond thin pretext that as a Galilean, Yeshua belonged to Herod's jurisdiction.

No matter what Herod's verdict might be in this matter, Pilate sliced a pallid smile, *I shall be absolved of all responsibility in this matter.* But things had not gone according to plan when Herod returned Yeshua to Pilate for a pronouncement. The carpenter was now back in Pilate's courtyard, with a crowd of angry black buzzards circling in ceremonial robes.

A pomegranate breeze feathered the hair at Pilate's temples, which circled into gray ringlets in the heat. Gaius and his troops remained at inelastic attention. Red with rage and indignation, Jewish religious leaders shrieked and taunted. The scarlet and gold banners of Rome snapped in a tense, terse sky. A solitary sheep bleated somewhere in the blue distance.

The Jews have a ritual ceremony they perform when the body of a man who has been murdered is discovered and the killer cannot be identified. The elders gather and recite an ancient prayer: *Be merciful, O Lord, to Your people Yisrael, whom You have redeemed, and do not lay innocent blood upon them.* Then they all wash their hands ceremonially.

Pilate turned aside and spoke to a servant, "Bring me a basin of water." When the servant returned with a silver basin, Pilate dipped his hands into the water with deliberation as cold as the water. The liquid bit his fingers first, and then his palms and his wrists as the procurator tried to wash away his guilt. Pilate shook off the water and dried his hands on a towel, trying to wipe away not the evil he did, but the kindness he did not do.

"I am innocent of the blood of this just man. Look you to it." Pilate declared, beckoning to Gaius, who raised his right arm in an imperial salute and shouted, "Hail, Caesar!"

The withered Valley of Hinnom sampled the breeze yet again. A viper awaiting its prey, the potter's field paused, probing. Anticipating. Yeshua of Nazareth peered sadly at both the procurator and the centurion as Pilate barked at Gaius, "Crucify this prisoner with those thieves I condemned yesterday."

Thirty-eight

Had it happened so quickly? Gaius was already familiar with the chronology of events, but his rank-and-order mind ticked off the proceedings from a military perspective.

There were two trials, one before the Sanhedrin, and one before Pilate, the Roman governor. Judea was subject to Rome. The Sanhedrin could not execute a death sentence without Pilate's consent. There were three stages in each trial, six in all.

Yeshua's arrest took place outside the old city in the olive orchard near midnight. The first stage of his "trial" was before Annas. The pensive, tight-lipped father-in-law of Caiaphas had been deposed from the high priesthood by the Romans, but was still regarded by many as the true high priest. At any rate, Annas managed to accrue fabulous wealth through reportedly shady dealings in the temple trading booths. Sparse, sardonic and with as much diplomatic skill as a pit viper, Annas may not have been the high priest any more, but the wizened raisin of a man still retained a sizable chunk of the office's influence.

Following a futile interview with the braying donkey that was Annas, Yeshua was hauled to the house of Caiaphas for his main Jewish trial. The sham of an ecclesiastical night trial, illegal by the Jews' own law, ended after a cock crowed and a rose-lipped sunrise kissed the Yerushalayim hills. The Sanhedrin could not hold a legal session at night, so a special session convened at daybreak to issue a death sentence. In fact, the Sanhedrin officially ratified its midnight decision to charge Yeshua with "blasphemy" early Friday, affording their "trial" a gaunt appearance of legality.

"Naturally," Gaius reasoned in retrospect, mind pumping like a galley bilge, "this religious charge would carry as much weight with Pilate as a black gnat on a silver stallion."

Sanhedrin members knew this, too. Clustered in groups of three or four or more, heads shook, backs stiffened and eyes flashed at Yeshua, spearing him with hateful stares. A few feeble protestations were shoved aside. The majority of members concocted something which would make the brutal, buzzard-like procurator sit up and take notice: a charge of sedition against Rome.

The etheric atmosphere of Pilate's courtyard wheezed and whispered as Yeshua stood before Pilate just after daybreak, barefoot on a rough flagstone courtyard while a laconic Pilate tossed accusations in his face like stones. Yeshua made no reply to the Sanhedrin's charges. Pilate took him within the palace for a private interview.

As shrewd as a money-lender and as slippery as lamp oil, Pilate faced the bloody carpenter and wondered, *This charge of sedition is as trumped up and inflated as an old wineskin bursting with fresh wine. The accusation will surely explode, collapse of its own dim-witted dullness.* He was somewhat startled when it did not.

"From Galilee, he is?" Gaius recalled Pilate's grating voice as the procurator grasped at the straw, hoping to weave from it a ladder to escape the rapidly rising political mire. "Send him to Herod" Pilate snapped, "Herod Antipas has jurisdiction over all matters Galilean. Get him out of here," Pilate strode from the room, glad to be free "from that troublesome meddler."

Thirty-nine

Crouching outside Yerushalayim, a little hill raises its bleak head. A ragged outcropping of rock squatting outside the city's northwestern wall near the Damascus gate, it is called *Golgotha*. The 'place of the skull.' It is a rock ledge, some thirty feet high, just above 'Jeremias' Grotto.' Huddled around the barren brow of this knoll, four women clutched each other and wept.

Old Hadessa's sturdy arms coiled around Yo-hannah, her lamb. A lady of rank and privilege, Yo-hannah clutched at Hadessa's sleeve and dissolved into tears. A Samaritan woman's arms wound about her, too. Chava, the lost sheep from a despised flock, had tried to return a kindness, offering a gourd of water to Yeshua as he climbed the desolate hill of Golgotha: *Do you remember me, the woman from the well? Remember when you asked me for a drink?*

The gourd was dashed out of Chava's hand by a gruff Roman centurion, but not before Yeshua's eyes met hers. A world of understanding passed between the shepherd and the sheep in that one moment. *Were you maligned, Chava? Despised? Rejected? Abandoned?*

"Yes," the sad eyes said. "I know. I am." Chava's eyes rimmed with tears at the recollection as she crowded into the throng of four. Clutching Chava's hand, Veronica wiped her cheeks. A river of tears streamed down Veronica's formerly gaunt, lined face, newly smoothed and rounded by health and wholeness. Moved with pity, Veronica gave Yeshua her handkerchief that he might wipe his forehead as Yeshua carried his cross to Skull Rock. *I touched the fringe of your garment. I have not forgotten your healing.*

Each woman had been restored, made new by the bloodied, beaten man whose own flesh was now torn and shredded, soaked with humiliation and shame.

The stalwart, hulking frame of old Hadessa hovered around the sobbing trio. Holding Yo-hannah's fingers, the old woman flung wide her arms and enveloped the Samaritan woman, then pulled the once-unclean-but-purified Veronica inside her grandmotherly embrace. They were her family now. All of them.

A sinister gloom lathered the hillside. As Gaius and his troops neared the disreputable field, they were met by the acrid smell of smoke hanging over its smoldering corruptions. Gaius initially rued the last four goblets of wine he had doused down his throat at the insistence of an older, more seasoned soldier, "No sober man should ever have this task." As the Roman from Derbe marched three condemned men and his detachment out of the city past the reeking, garbage-strewn field before him, Gaius had second thoughts about the wine.

Maybe I should've had more, Gaius considered, his legs a bit wobbly but still obediently moving forward toward a narrow thread of path up a little knoll. At the crest stood three crosses sans cross beams. He had his orders. Spikes, hammers, screams, and three men hung in an angry black sky waiting to die.

A small crowd followed the condemned men out of the city and gathered on the hillside. Gaius kept his bloodshot eyes on the pathetic little groupings—most were shabbily dressed, many were weeping. He did not expect any trouble but dispatched his soldiers among the people where they stood leaning on their lances, surly and reeking of wine.

A quartet of female mourners caught Gaius' eye. Three youngish women, one dressed in silk and jewelry denoting a lady of distinction, another dressed as a Samaritan, and a third with sad, soft eyes. They all raised tear-streaked faces toward the center cross. Surrounding the three younger women was a husky, big-boned woman with a flint-like visage. Old Hadessa's strong, seasoned arms served as supports and sentinels for the distraught trio of younger women.

Gaius looked sharply at the sky. It was barely noon, yet the heavens were creped in black. The earth rumbled and lurched. Regaining his footing with no small amount of effort, Gaius returned to a small cadre of soldiers. A leather dice cup was shaken, passed from one pair of hands to another. Gaius' head ached and his lips were cracked. He joined the group and tossed out the dice, "What are we playing for this time?" A soldier nodded toward the foot of the center cross, where a homespun outer garment, a brown robe, lay in a crumpled heap.

"Here, let me look at that" Gaius gestured at the robe. A laconic legionnaire retrieved the garment and tossed it to Gaius. It was a fine robe, woven by the steady hands of a Galilean woman, a well-loved former slave. Its hem was once touched in faith by an infirm woman.

"He won't need it anymore," Gaius shrugged, folding the garment over his arm.

The other soldiers eyed the robe. Seamless, it was woven in a single piece from top to bottom and thus too valuable to be cut up or torn. "Let's toss for it. High number wins" Gaius offered, shaking the leather dice cup. A few minutes later the Roman from Derbe was the new owner of a seamless Galilean robe.

The darkness deepened. A cacophony of euphonious noises pummeled Skull Hill: moans from dying men. Rattling dice. Cursing soldiers. Pharisees jeering. Women sobbing. Amid the hubbub an agonizing cry escaped Yeshua, as if he was begging, or perhaps roaring, at a distant friend.

Forty

Gaius had seen men crucified, pressed his knee into forearms and shins and driven spikes through hands and feet. But he had never seen any man die like this one. *That Unknown God of Arieh's,* Gaius pondered. *The One with no name.*

"What is this prisoner's name?" Gaius croaked, motioning toward the center cross. He wanted to be sure.

"He is called Yeshua of Nazareth."

Staring upward, Gaius squared his shoulders and rubbed his jaw. It was almost as if this Yeshua died voluntarily, laying down his life as an act of his will. A choice. A memory stirred, something Arieh once claimed. What was it? The Name used of no one but Yisrael's God? The One who is. The One who causes. The One who loves enough to ...? *You told us your name...*

Gaius looked up again. He couldn't help wondering. *Maybe this God of Arieh's has a name after all. Maybe,* Gaius pondered, *this God of Love is unknown no longer. Yes, I've worshipped idols. But if this Nameless God is the only god and I have offended him by worshipping other deities, what can I do to gain his favor?*

Gaius rubbed unshaved morning stubble with the back of his hand and pondered. *Can it be? This man has lost everything. The Jews, in their trial, mocked him. Herod and his soldiers mocked him and so did Pilate's. Now even the priests, scribes and elders of his own people mock him.*

Gaius leaned a hand against the Roman timber and looked up. He drew back his hand. It dripped blood. He wiped the red stain off on his tunic, leaving a smear. Gaius could not wipe away the icy shivers that gnawed at his spine.

It's as if he willingly emptied himself of everything: his family and friends, his honor, his reputation, vocation, possessions. Everything. Even his life. He gave up <u>*everything*</u> *for this cross. Why?*

Gaius glanced at Yeshua's robe, lying in a crumpled heap on the arid, irascible ground. *And this homespun cloak, the last remnant of his earthly possessions? Even that doesn't belong to him now.* As the hard centurion peered and pondered, the hard crust of cynicism and doubt fell away like abandoned armor, and he remembered.

Can Skull Rock be the place where vertical holiness intersects a horizontal crossbeam of...? What had Arieh claimed about his Unknown God? The God with No Name, the God who... loves?

The centurion looked closer. Arieh said something else, something about how God can only be comprehended by the spirit. *"Those who wish to know Him must come to Him by ... faith?" Yes, that was it.*

Gaius wiped a grimy hand across his tunic. Staring upward at the center cross with bloodshot eyes, the centurion stepped back. In that wretched, rumbling darkness a heart full of suspicion, skepticism and self coagulated within the seasoned solider. A stab of lightning slit the sky. A sliver of light flickered inside Gaius: "Surely this was a righteous man."

Forty-one

Can you hear us, Merciful One?
Are You listening, Giver of Grace?

"How could it come to this?" Yo-hannah choked, voicing the thoughts of her unlikely comrades. The women looked on helplessly as Yeshua's life blood drained out, the crimson conclusion to a good man's life.

Hadessa understood. Passover. Righteous wrath. Doomed humanity. A condemned lamb. A penal substitution. Ransom. *He was a surrendered sacrifice, but never once an impotent prey.*

You told us Your name, how You must long to be close to us. For a price.

The parcel of ground known as the Field of Blood was purchased by the priests with the thirty pieces of silver which Judah *ish keriot* cast down in the temple. A plot of ground bought with the price of blood, it was the place where Judah hanged himself.

Akeldama. Field of Blood. Blood sacrifice demanded for atonement, for purification. For redemption from an eternal Akeldama, a potter's field of souls lost for eternity.

... The punishment that brought us peace was upon him, and by his wounds we are healed. ... And the Lord has laid on him the iniquity of us all.

Like the River Jordan, the Lamb of God descended, but not

from Mount Hermon. From heaven. He took up human form and dwelt among men. Being a man, he bled. Was his blood the ultimate answer to Akeldama, the Ultimate Passover? Blood of the Lamb: the price of pardon? What needed to be done, he did, making a way for internal purity and eternal deliverance. No more goats or bulls. No more earthly high priests.

Near Skull Rock a sheep bleated. A moment later, The Sacrifice surrendered. Then It was finished. Demand satisfied. Legal requirements met. The transaction completed, the covenant sealed by the death of him that made it.

A veil of separation inside the temple rent into an open door. A new high priest, a once-for-all sacrifice parted the path. The Old yielded to the New.

~

It was evening, the day before Shabbat. Yosef approached Pilate with his request. A tall, angular man from the Judean city of Arimathea, the wealthy Yosef was a secret follower of Yeshua and a reputable member of the Sanhedrin. He had not assented to their counsel and deed concerning Yeshua.

"May I take away the body of Yeshua?"

"Is he dead so soon?" Pilate sent for Gaius and inquired of the morose centurion.

"Yes," Gaius replied unsteadily, "that Galilean has been dead for some time."

"You may take the body," Pilate waved Yosef away, glad to be done with the deed.

Counting out silver at the bazaar later, Yosef bought a cloth of fine linen. He then met another secret follower of Yeshua, Nicodemus. It was heart-rending, gruesome work. Conducted with grief too deep for words, the silent pair gently removed Yeshua's body from the cross, wrapped it in clean linen cloth with fragrant myrrh and aloes, according to the Jewish custom, and placed the body in a garden tomb near that wretched hill. It was the Preparation Day, Friday, and because Shabbat was coming on the body had to be taken care of quickly. Hearts aching, Yosef and

Nicodemus and others heaved a great stone against the door of the tomb and departed, helpless and hopeless.

The men were not alone in their grief. A little band of tearful, red-eyed women followed them and saw the tomb and how Yeshua's body was laid in it. Numbered among the somber troupe were the gracious Yo-hannah, the healed Veronica, and the restored Chava.

~

Now it was early on the first day of the week. Crippled hunks of sky flapped and sagged in the limp morning air. Dull clouds swathed the horizon like celestial grave clothes. Brown sparrows lamented the events of Friday and Saturday from drooping palm fronds.

A feckless sunrise creased the dawn as Yo-hannah, Chava, and Veronica stumbled toward the tomb in silence, carrying spices and perfumes. It was early when they started, and still dark.

If anyone had reason to sleep in this morning, was it not this unhappy trio? *Besides*, Chava thought, *it's dangerous to go outside. Yeshua has just been killed at the insistence of a rabid vigilante mob. They're certainly looking for his followers. Maybe we should just stay inside? After all,* Chava sniffed, *the master is dead. It's not like we're going to miss anything.*

Somehow her feet plodded forward with the others. The acrid aroma of dead dreams and shattered hope filled nostrils, mouths, and hearts to retching level.

~

"Now?" Hadessa shot the query heavenward like an arrow loosed from its quiver. "Is today The Day?"

The question had hung on the old woman's tongue for years. Decades. Millenia. It was on her lips when she sang to a group of startled shepherds as part of a midnight multitude. Since the slaughter of the innocents at Bethlehem. And long ago, when she was commanded to guard the entrance to a beautiful garden with a flaming sword, lest a newly evicted couple attempt to return.

So many years. Such a long wait. Centuries of waiting. Waiting through disobedience, a flood, captivities, destructions and reconstructions, prophets, priests and kings. And years ago, dispatched into this tired, ancient form as guardian of a good woman's daughter.

"Now, El Elyon, O Holy One of Yisrael? These children of yours see only death and despair. Look! They bring burial spices as if this death is the end, permanent!"

Hadessa's choir colleagues burst into song in response to a divine roar! Fresh strength surged into gnarled limbs, straightened a bent back, unfurled sturdy arms. Her raiment dazzled with the blinding light of a long-ago reflection. She wore a shining belt that sheathed a gleaming sword. Face goldened and glowing, her eyes blazed like fire as she burst into a brand new *Hallel!*

Forty-two

Neither man knew it at the time, but Gaius and Julius were soon to part ways and then reconnect in a manner neither of them would have dared fathom.

New orders arrived from Rome for Gaius. He returned to Galatia to oversee the construction of an aqueduct. It was there that he came to know the owner of the robe which he won in a game of chance at the foot of a Roman cross. It was where the former centurion gained his *liberti* and joined the ranks of other "freedmen" who became so by the initiative of Another, no longer Unknown.

In Galatia Gaius thought often of Arieh and his "loving God," at long last realizing that his young armor-bearer was not really "gone" after all. There would be a reunion some day, and on that day Gaius would hear Arieh tell how he returned to his country and became an important treasury official under Candace, Queen of the Nubians. Arieh would tell how he had traveled to Yerushalyim to worship and on his homeward journey he read aloud from the prophet Isaias in his chariot. Overheard by a follower of Yeshua, the man had asked, "Do you understand what you are reading?"

"How can I?" Arieh replied, "unless someone explains it to me?" The former armor bearer hoisted Philip into the chariot. Together, they read:

He was led like a sheep to the slaughter, and as a lamb

before the shearer is silent, so he did not open his mouth. In his humiliation he was deprived of justice. Who can speak of his descendants? For his life was taken from the earth.

"Tell me, please, who is the prophet talking about, himself or someone else?"

Philip slung his coarse robe over his shoulder and grinned. "He's talking about someone else. Someone else, indeed." Thus *Arieh*, the lion, found his God of Love, was baptized, and went home to Nubia rejoicing.

Perhaps Gaius was pondering a reunion with Arieh when he joined Sopater, son of Pyrrhus from Berea, Aristarchus and Secundus from Thessalonica, a youngish lad named Timothy from Lystra, Tychicus, from the province of Asia, and Trophimus, an Ephesian Gentile. Together, the group accompanied a man from Tarsus on his journeys throughout Macedonia, Philippi and Troas, teaching and spreading the word about the man whose robe Gaius still bore.

Julius, on the other hand, finally received his orders to return to Rome as part of the Imperial Regiment. As an imperial courier, his specific duties included delivering prisoners for trial. It was during one of these "deliveries" that the centurion met a peculiar prisoner, a vociferous Jew, frail in body but with steel in his soul. Shipwrecked en route to Italy, Julius saved the man's life from overzealous soldiers more willing to drown than to lose prisoners. Every soldier knew that if a prisoner escaped under his charge, the guard's life was taken in his place. Julius knew this, too.

"Hold!" Julius barked at a soldier whose steel blade pressed Paul's throat. There was something about the small, unimpressive man that made Julius uneasy. Whatever it was, Julius was charged with delivering his prisoners alive to Rome, shipwreck or not. The subordinate soldier saluted smartly and returned his sword to its sheath.

"Everyone who can swim, jump overboard and head for land" Julius ordered. "The rest of you, grab a plank or a piece of the ship--anything that floats--and make for shore." Everyone eventually reached *terra firma* on the island of Malta, the same place where Julius met *terra firma* of the soul. But before that came the Dawn.

Forty-three

Yo-hannah met Veronica and Chava, each carrying a bundle of spices and ointments which they had prepared to anoint Yeshua's dead body. Yo-hannah was perplexed, vaguely distracted by the sudden disappearance of Hadessa. She looked everywhere, but the faithful old woman was no where to be found.

A priest mounted the temple ramparts and blew a silver trumpet. The blast announced the dawn of a new day and the opening of the temple gates. *Shararit*, the dawn service, began with the priests presenting barley bread in the temple according to Torah and the law of tithing and firstfruits.

Shavuot. The giving of Torah. *Succoth*. The giving of first fruits. The singing of the *Hallel*.

~

"Now!" came the divine imperative, and the being who was Hadessa hastened to obey. The ground shook as the radiant being that was once an old woman hurtled the stone from the tomb. Hadessa sat upon the stone and waited, her disguise at long last cast aside.

Nearing the tomb, the women saw that the stone had been removed somehow and looked around, frightened. They saw no evidence of Roman or other tampering with the sealed sepulcher, yet it was open.

Her brow beaded with sweat, Veronica exhaled in ragged huffs. *Haven't I been frightened before? Who did I call upon then? Did he not hear? Did he not answer?* She stopped, eyes welling. *But he cannot hear, nor can he answer now...*

The women entered the cave trembling and timorous, sensing something was dreadfully, extraordinarily amiss. They had to stoop to enter. Hewn out of rock, the musty, damp crypt was no more than four feet high. Sandals slipped on rough floor. Fingers shook. Adjusting to the gloom, three sets of eyes peered around the sepulcher, astonished and afraid.

"Where is his body?" Yo-hannah looked around, numb, disbelieving. "Where have they taken him?" She combed the cobwebs of her mind and unearthed a hazy recollection about Yerushalayim, betrayal, mockery and death. What had Yeshua said about the "third day?"

The body was not in the tomb, but two dazzling beings were. One spoke. "Do not fear," the former Hadessa assured the trembling trio. "Why do you seek the living one among the dead? He is not here, for he has risen, as he said. Come, see..."

The light being caught Yo-hannah's eye and smiled. Was it Yo -hannah's imagination, or did this "light being" seem to say, *Have no fear, my lamb; your little ones are no longer lost. They are with the One you seek, the One who saved your son at the seashore. Don't you know that He has saved you, too?*

Yo-hannah gulped. Veronica gasped. Chava stood mute. Terrified out of their wits, the trio turned tail and fled. Finding the big fisherman and Yo-hannan, the women wrung their hands and cried, "They took away the Lord from the sepulcher! We don't know where they laid him." Barely intelligible gibberish punctuated by snatches of "angels" and "empty" accompanied their astonishing narrative.

Petros, "the rock," and Yo-hannan, "the beloved disciple," raced back to the tomb with the women. Yo-hannan outran the big fisherman but it was Symeon Petros who rushed in, looked around and found the cave empty just as the women said.

Adjusting to the gloom, Petros' eyes closed on something. Two heaps lay on the empty stone slab. Two heaps of cloth.

Nothing else, except for charred rock on the wall. A divine detonation?

Petros' jaw unhinged in awed amazement. He stared at the linen cloths which were lying by themselves, and the napkin, which had been about Yeshua's head--not lying with the linen cloths but folded up in a place by itself!

Yo-hannan darted inside next and took in the sepulcher, speechless. He reemerged into the cold morning light, clearly shaken but grinning an enigmatic smile that the others couldn't read.

Chava held back outside the tomb, uncertain and afraid. Her face red and blotchy, she stooped and looked into the sepulcher. Two dazzling beings sat inside, one at the head and the other at the feet where the body of Yeshua had lain. Sniffling and incredulous, Chava wiped her eyes, turned around and began to flee. Someone stood behind her, but she couldn't make out the face.

"Woman, why are you weeping?"

"Because they took away my Lord, and I know not where they laid him."

"Woman, why are you weeping" he repeated gently. "Whom are you seeking?"

Who am I seeking?! Who could make a half-breed whole? Who could know all about me and not bury me beneath a mountain of shame—shame I myself earned and deserved? Who could open heaven to a despised Samaritan? His name was Yeshua. I thought he was Mashiah. My deliverer, my king. I thought he was... maybe he was...

Supposing this man to be the gardener, Chava mumbled, "Sir, if you bore him away, tell me where you laid him, and I will take him away."

"Chava" he replied. One word. Her *name* caught in a sunbeam. He said it just like he used to--softly, cocooned in *chesed* --and she knew.

YESHUA!

The Name above every name! The condemnation crusher. The reviver of the dead. Supporter of the fallen. Healer of the afflicted.

Freer of the bound, cleanser of the soiled. The sole son of his *Abba.*

Chava heard the flap of Galilean homespun and breathed the lavish fragrance of *chesed*, poured out by the one whose ears and arms are ever open. Yo-hannah and Veronica joined her, gaping at first, then laughing, jumping, crying tears of joy!

Who is like unto thee, who keepest thy faith to them that sleep in the dust, Lord of the mightiest of mighty acts?

Yes-hua smiled. *Yes. I AM.* Immutable. Changeless. Faithful. The only Son of the Son-sender. The Heavenly Descender. *Buried in humanity up to my eye brows, I strode into the dark abyss of death and reemerged in victory!*

Could it be? The impossible wrapped in the incredible burst into the morning, first witnessed by a trio of... *women?* Yo-hannah knew what it was to lose a son. She had lost four of them. She also knew that her only son, Rephaiah, would have perished at the Galilean seashore had it not been for Him.

YES-hua!

So it was that on this morning a new First Fruit was given. Neither flute nor harp, reed nor cymbal could accompany the new song. A fresh song, a come-and-see tune rose with the sun.

"Empty! Yeshua's grave is *empty!* He is *alive*!!"

YES-hua!

Revival? Support? Healing, freeing, faithing, mighty acts? The sweet and tender mercy of racham? Veronica dragged herself from past to present. *When? Where? From whom?*

I AM the sin-shoulderer, the risen lamb! I AM the devil-defeater, the death-defier! I AM! The potter's field purchased by the serpent-smasher. I gave up everything to call you by name, to offer my *Name to all who ask.*

YES-hua!

Chava: *Mercy-ed.* Veronica: Vera-icon. *True image.* Rephaiah: *Yahweh has healed.* Yo-hannah: *Yahweh is gracious.*

Each name a rescued one. Reclaimed, renewed, restored! Redeemed. Remembered by The Name that never forgets.

Akeldama exchanged for Assurance.

The women chorused their new *Hallel* like a heavenly choir: *Come and see the Finisher who forces the snake of this world to let His people go!*

Their paean of praise ricocheted off the Yerushalayim hills, roared off the Kidron, ripped through the Valley of Hinnom, and rang throughout the whole world.

~

For all who call upon the Name today, the heavenly *Hallel* still rings.

SOURCES

Aldrete, Gregory S.: "Daily Life in the Roman City." *Daily Life Online: Exploring Everyday Life Past and Present.* Greenwood Publishing Group, 2005.

_____. "Political Life: Weapons, Rome." *Daily Life Online: Exploring Everyday Life Past and Present.* Greenwood Publishing Group, 2005.

_____. "The Ancient World: Weapons of Rome." *Daily Life Online: Exploring Everyday Life Past and Present.* Greenwood Publishing Group, 2005.

Berkhof, L.: *Systematic Theology.* Grand Rapids, MI: Wm. B. Eerdmans Publishing Co., 1939.

Bishop, Jim: *The Day Christ Died*: New York, Harper, 1957.

_____. *The Day Christ was Born*: New York, Harper, 1977.

Brown, Raymond E., *The Death of the Messiah: From Gethsemane to the Grave; A Commentary on the Passion Narratives in the Four Gospels*, 2 vols. Doubleday, 1994.

Bryan, Alton T., ed.: *The New Compact Bible Dictionary.* Grand Rapids, MI: Zondervan Publishing House, 1967.

Bull, Robert J. and Crisler, B. Cobbey: *Come See The Place: The Holy Land Jesus Knew.* Englewood Cliffs, N.J.: Prentice-Hall, Inc., 1978.

Bultmann, Rudolf, *Jesus and the Word.* Tr. by Louise Pettibone Smith and Erminie Huntress Lantero (1934; reprint, Scribner, 1982.)

Charlesworth, James J., ed., *Jesus' Jewishness: Exploring the Place of Jesus within Early Judaism.* Am. Interfaith Inst. Crossroad, 1991.

Cheney, Johnston M: *The Life of Christ in Stereo.* Portland, OR: Multnomah Press, 1969.

Connolly, Peter: *Jews in the Time of Jesus.* Oxford: Oxford University Press, 1994.

Converse, Gordon N.: *Come see the place: the Holy Land Jesus Knew.* Englewood Cliffs, NJ: 1978.

Daniel-Rops, Henri: *Daily Life in Palestine at the Time of Christ.* Hachette, Paris: English translation by Weidenfeld & Nicholson, 1961.

Davis, John D., and Gehman, Henry Synder: *The Westminster Dictionary of the Bible*. Philadelphia: Westminster Press, 1944.

Degert, Antoine: *Saint Veronica, The Catholic Encyclopedia,* Volume XV, New York, NY, 2005.

DeJonge, Marinus de: *Jesus, the Servant-Messiah.* Yale University Press, 1991.

Dunn, James D.G.: *Jesus Remembered.* Eerdmans, 2003.

Elizondo, Virgilio P.: *A God of Incredible Surpises: Jesus of Galilee.* Rowman & Littlefield, 2003.

Fowler, Gary: University of Kentucky, *Tiberias*, Encyclopedia Americana. Grolier Online, 2006.

Gower, Ralph: *The New Manners and Customs of Bible Times*. Chicago, IL: Moody Press, 1987.

Gromacki, Robert G.: *New Testament Survey*. Grand Rapids, MI: Baker Book House, 1974.

Grant, Frederick C.: Union Theological Seminary, N.Y., *Galilee, Sea Of,* Encyclopedia Americana. Grolier Online, 2006.

Halley, Henry H.: *Halley's Bible Handbook.* Grand Rapids, MI: Zondervan Publishing House, 1965.

Harrison, Everett F: *Introduction to the New Testament*. Grand Rapids, MI: Eerdmans Publishing Company, 1971.

Henry, Carl F.H, ed.: *The Biblical Expositor: The Living Theme of the Great Book, Volumes Two* and *Three.* Philadelphia: A.J. Holman Company, 1960.

___, ed.: *Basic Christian Doctrines*. Grand Rapids, MI: Baker Book House, 1962.

Hepper, Nigel. *Lands of the Bible: From Plants and Creatures to Battles and Covenants*. Oxford, England: Lion Publishing plc., 1995.

Hughes, Kent. *The Gift.* Wheaton, Ill, Crossway Books, 1994.

Keyes, Nelson B.: *Story of the Bible World in Map, Word and Picture.* Pleasantville, New York: Reader's Digest Association, 1962.

Kraeling, Emil G: *Bible Atlas*. New York: Rand McNally and Company, 1952.

Josephus: *War*, V.5.3.

Lockyer, Herbet*: All the Women of the Bible.* Grand Rapids, MI: Zondervan, 1967.

Lowder, Chris: Bible scholar, proofreader, fact checker, cultural consultant, "bouncer-off-er," Greek translator, "right arm" and all-around good guy.

Marshall, I. Howard*: The Origins of New Testament Christology*, rev. ed. Inter-Varsity Press, 1991.

Matthews, Victor H.*: Manners and Customs in the Bible*. Peabody, MA: Hendrickson Publishers, Inc., 1991.

McClymond, Michael J., *Familiar Stranger: An Introduction to Jesus of Nazareth.* Eerdmans, 2004.

Merrill, Eugene H.: *An Historical Survey of the Old Testament*. Grand Rapids, MI: Baker Book House, 1966.

Mills, James R.: *Memoirs of Pontius Pilate.* Grand Rapids, MI: Fleming H. Revell, 2000.

Charles F. and Harrison, Everett F., ed.*: The New Testament and Wycliffe Bible Commentary.* Chicago: Moody Press, 1973.

Porter, J.R.: *Jesus Christ: the Jesus of History, the Christ of Faith.* New York: Oxford University Press, 1999.

Punton, Anne: *The World Jesus Knew*. Grand Rapids, MI: Monarch Books, 1996.

Readers Digest Association: *Jesus and His Times*. Pleasantville, NY: Readers Digest Association, 1987.

Sanders, E. P.,: *The Historical Figure of Jesus*. 1933; reprint, Penguin, 1996.

Sauer, Erich: *In the Arena of Faith: A Call to a Consecrated Life.* Grand Rapids, MI: Wm. B. Eerdmans Publishing Company, 1956.

___, *The Triumph of the Crucified: A Historical Revelation in the New Testament*. Grand Rapids, MI: Wm. B. Eerdmans Publishing Company, 1955.

Sobel, Rabbi B., Temple Emanu-El, New York City, *Galilee*, Encyclopedia Americana. Grolier Online, 2006.

Spurgeon, Charles H.: *My Sermon Notes: Matthew to Acts*. Grand Rapids, MI: Baker Book House, first published 1884; reprinted 1981.

Stalker, James.: *The Trial and Death of Jesus Christ*. Grand Rapids, MI: Zondervan Publishing House, 1961.

Tenney, Merrill C.: *New Testament Survey*: Grand Rapids, MI: Eerdmans Publishing Company, 1961.

Van Voorst, Robert E.: *Jesus Outside the New Testament: An Introduction to the Ancient Evidence*. Eerdmans, 2000.

Vermes, Geza: *Jesus in His Jewish Context*. Fortress Press, 2003.

Watson, G.R.: *The Roman Soldier*. Ithaca, N.Y.: Cornell University Press, 1969.

Webster, G.: *The Roman Imperial Army of the First and Second Centuries*. 3rd ed. Totowa, N.J.: Barnes and Noble, 1985.

Weiss, Christian G.: *Insights Into Bible Times and Customs*. Lincoln, NE: The Good News Broadcasting Association, Inc., 1972.

Wiley, H. Orton: *Christian Theology, Volumes I and II.* Kansas City, MO: Beacon Hill Press, 1941.

Wright, Nicholas T.: *The Original Jesus: The Life and Vision of a Revolutionary.* Grand Rapids, MI: Eerdmans, 1996.

A native southern Californian, *Kristine Lowder* was born and raised in San Diego. She said "yes" to Yeshua on Easter Sunday 1967, following an Easter lesson by her third grade Sunday school teacher, Mrs. Eleanor Jermain.

Kristine attributes her California home church, Covenant Presbyterian, and Christian camping experiences at Hume Lake and Forest Home for launching much of her early Christian growth. She's had a heart for children's ministry and Christian camping ever since.

A 1982 graduate of Biola University, Kristine moved to Washington with her husband and their four sons in 2002. They enjoy hiking, camping, exploring and birding amid the beautiful Cascades.

Akeldama is Kristine's first historical novel. She's working on her next title.

www.ingramcontent.com/pod-product-compliance
Lightning Source LLC
Chambersburg PA
CBHW071311200626
46813CB00015B/1466
* 9 7 8 1 8 8 5 0 5 4 7 4 6 *